KU-038-011

CONTENTS

was quitting my top executive job, I'd been bombarded with reactions ranging from outright disbelief to horrified disapproval, especially when people heard what I was exchanging my high-flying corporate career *for*. I really didn't feel like justifying myself all over again.

The stewardess stopped by our seats and offered us a tray of drinks. I selected an orange juice whilst my companion helped herself to two glasses of white wine. She gave me an embarrassed look, tinged with defiance.

"I know they say you shouldn't really drink in the air but I find it helps to settle my nerves," she said with an awkward laugh.

She certainly seemed to need to settle her nerves. Over the next few hours, as we made our way across the Indian Ocean, had a stopover in Dubai, then continued on to London, I noticed that the glasses of wine kept coming. The woman drank like a fish.

It's none of my business, I reminded myself firmly. *I have enough troubles of my own without sticking my nose in anyone else's.* I handed my finished meal to the smiling stewardess and folded the tray into the seatback in front of me. Jenn had already reclined her seat and seemed to be sleeping, with an eye-mask across her face. I followed suit, leaning back and closing my eyes as they dimmed the lights in the cabin.

I can't believe I'm really going back... eight years... somehow it's gone so quickly... and yet it feels longer too... Well, I always thought I'd go back some day but not like this... It's weird to think of how life is going to change... no more lazy Sunday mornings at the cafés in Paddington, no more barbecues at the beach, no more blazing sunshine and sparkling blue harbour... That view of the city from my gorgeous penthouse apartment... oh, I'm going to miss that... but no, that apartment isn't mine anymore...

Yes, I thought, opening my eyes. That gorgeous penthouse apartment was now a lump of cold, hard cash in my bank account, together with the rest of my savings—my little nest egg, carefully saved up all these years—not so little anymore, actually. And yet, still barely enough...

The dreaded thoughts whirled inside my head: *Am I doing the right thing? Am I? Everyone thinks I'm crazy... giving up what I had, risking all my savings... all for what—a sudden impulse and a silly dream? I'm twenty-nine, too old for silly dreams... Dreams are for seven-year-olds, when you still believed in unicorns and fairy tale endings...* I stared blindly into the darkened cabin around me. *Oh God, have I made a terrible mistake?*

I sighed and shut my eyes again, forcing the thoughts away. *Stop. It's done now. And you did do the right thing. The first right thing you've done in a long time. You'll see... It'll be fine... There are still fairy tale endings sometimes...*

My thoughts drifted, blurred, faded... and then suddenly, I was being gently shaken awake. I sat up slowly to find the smiling stewardess next to me once more, offering a tray of drinks. I looked around, blinking. The lights were back on in the cabin and people were standing, stretching, or ambling down the aisle to join the queue for the toilets. A baby wailed inconsolably somewhere nearby. Next to me, Jenn stretched stiffly and stifled a yawn.

"I can't believe I slept most of the way," I said, rubbing the crick in my neck. "I must have been more exhausted than I realised." I glanced at Jenn, who looked tired and drawn. "Did you manage to sleep okay?"

"No," Jenn said in a low voice. She swallowed, then said, "There was horrible turbulence..."

"Really?" I looked at her in surprise. "I have to say, I didn't even notice it."

She stared at me. "How can you not notice it? Every time the plane dips and bumps around... and your stomach does that awful lurching thing... I think—" Her voice cracked and she swallowed again, convulsively. "I just know we're going to crash—"

"Hey, hey..." I said gently, giving her an awkward pat on her arm. "You're just letting your imagination run away with you. You said so yourself—air travel is actually safer than driving in a car. The statistics don't lie."

She said nothing but swallowed nervously again. I gave her another thoughtful look. Was it normal to be this nervous of flying? And if so, why had she chosen to come on this trip? Most people with a real phobia of flying would usually avoid travelling by air. The last thing they would do is book themselves on a twenty-hour flight across the globe...

Breakfast was served and then, above our heads, a disembodied voice announced:

"Ladies and gentlemen, we have begun our descent and will shortly be landing at London Heathrow Airport. The weather in London is a chilly 13°C, 55°F, with a northerly wind and some rain expected. Please make sure that..."

"Is something the matter?" I asked as Jenn began searching frantically through the seat pocket in front of her.

"Oh, nothing... just... I tend to forget things so I wanted to make sure I hadn't left anything in the seat pocket before we land and there's that mad rush to get off the plane." She gave a self-deprecating smile. "I'd forget my own head if it wasn't screwed on. You won't believe how many umbrellas I've lost. I finally bought myself a raincoat with a hood because then at least that's attached to the coat."

She pulled a glasses case, a pair of socks, a packet of tissues, and a tourist guide to Oxford out of the pocket and stuffed them into her handbag, then hunted around under the seat for her shoes. Meanwhile, I was debating whether I'd have enough time to use the toilet, but it would have meant climbing over Jenn or asking her to get up to reach the aisle, and I decided I could wait until we landed. Instead, I turned to the window and felt a small thrill of excitement as the skyline of London came into view in the distance.

I'm coming home.

CHAPTER TWO

The plane landed as smoothly as it had taken off—although it seemed to be just as much an ordeal for Jenn, despite the amount of "nerve-steadying alcohol" she had consumed. In fact, she gripped the armrests so tightly, I thought she would wrench them off the seat, and her face was so white when we finally touched down that I began seriously wondering if I should have followed the instructions on the Safety Sheet and stuck an oxygen mask over her head. She breathed a huge sigh of relief as the plane finally taxied to a stop and the seatbelt sign was switched off.

As usual, there was a mad scramble as everyone suddenly seemed seized by a rabid desire to grab their bags and get off the plane. Jenn sprang up in the frenzy, dragging a trolley case out of the overhead compartment and shouldering her bag as she joined the line shuffling towards the nearest exit.

"Lovely to meet you. Hope you have a good trip back to Oxford!" she called over her shoulder as she hurried away.

I waved and smiled, then sat and waited until the initial stampede was over. Really, I didn't know what the mad rush was for: all those people pushing and jostling to get off first—and all that would happen is that they'd probably end up standing in the luggage hall, waiting in vain for their cases to arrive!

Getting up at a leisurely pace, I retrieved my own holdall from the overhead compartment and glanced over my shoulder to check that I hadn't left anything on the seat. That was when I noticed the scarf. It had been pushed down between the two seats and only the edge of the fringe showed. I reached over and pulled it out. It was a thick woollen scarf, in a bright turquoise pattern. It must have been Jenn's, I realised. She *had* forgotten something after all.

I glanced quickly down the aisle—it was empty now, except for a middle-aged gentleman who was slowly packing his briefcase—but I might still catch Jenn in the Luggage Hall. I was about to hurry off when something else caught my eye. A piece of paper sticking out of the seat pocket. I reached across and extracted it. It was a boarding pass with the name "J Murray" printed next to the seat number. Tucking it into my handbag, I hurried off the plane.

When I reached the Luggage Hall I was dismayed

to find that, for once, my cynical predictions had been wrong. The bags from my flight had arrived early and most of the passengers had already retrieved their luggage and gone through Customs. My own case was making its lonely way around the conveyor belt. I grabbed it and shoved it onto a nearby trolley, then looked around for Jenn but I couldn't see her anywhere. Sighing, I gave up and wheeled my trolley out into the Arrivals Hall. I had barely stepped out when I heard a familiar voice calling:

"Darling! Darling!"

I scanned the crowds and saw an elegant, middle-aged woman hurrying towards me. She was wearing a pale pink cashmere twinset and pearls, and had a vintage-style boxy handbag over one forearm, the way the Queen would hold it. In a hall full of people in frayed jeans and "travel loungewear" (read: shabby tracksuits), my mother stood out like a well-groomed poodle in a pack of scruffy mongrels.

"Darling!" She swooped in to give me a peck on the cheek.

"Hello, Mother," I said, returning her kiss.

"Darling! I've been counting the hours!" cried my mother.

I blinked. *Blimey.* I hadn't realised that my homecoming would mean so much to her. My mother was normally of the Old School and believed that a proper lady should never show her emotions too obviously in public. I hadn't seen her get this excited since Whittard of Chelsea brought out a Queen's Jubilee herbal tea range. *Still, I am her only child, so of course she would miss me terribly*, I thought smugly.

I reached out and squeezed her hand. "It's great to see you too, Mother—I didn't realise you were waiting so eagerly for me—"

"Well, of course, darling! I've been desperate for you to sort out my i-Tap. I just don't know what's wrong with it—I can turn it on but these strange little messages keep popping up on the screen... they're called Notifications, apparently, but I'm not sure what they're notifying me about. Something about an apple?"

I stifled a groan. I might have known that my mother's eagerness to see me was nothing to do with maternal love and more to do with technical desperation. Ever since she had followed her friends and bought an iPad a few weeks ago, I had been turned into Emergency IT Support and been bombarded with phone calls and messages at all times of day and night.

"Don't worry, Mother," I said. "I'll sort it out for you."

"Oh, thank goodness, because I'm becoming quite fond of my i-Tap. Do you know—you can play bridge on it and do crosswords... and Helen Green tells me that she even reads newspapers on it! You must show me how to do that on the i-Tap."

"I will—and it's an iPad, Mother. Not an i-Tap."

My mother looked at me in surprise. "But I am tapping."

"I know you're tapping but it's called a *pad*. Like a writing pad—except you tap on it."

"I do tap on the i-Tap," my mother insisted.

"No, no... I mean, yes, you *are* tapping but the thing you're tapping on is called a pad. You pad on the i-Tap... I mean... you tap on the iPad!" I growled, "Arrgh! Now you're mixing *me* up!"

"Don't worry, darling. I'm sure you'll get the hang of it. It can be a bit confusing in the beginning," my mother said kindly.

I ground my teeth and suddenly remembered why I went off to Australia in the first place. My mother chattered on, oblivious, as I followed her out to the car park. It wasn't until we were on the motorway that I remembered Jenn's scarf.

"Oh bollocks!" I said in annoyance.

My mother gasped. "Language, Gemma! Is that how you speak in Australia? A lady never swears or uses coarse language."

"Sorry, Mother," I muttered. "It's just that I picked up a scarf belonging to the lady sitting next to me on the plane. I meant to leave it at the airport Lost and Found, in case she called up looking for it. But I forgot and it's too late to go back now."

"Well, can't you post it to her?"

"I don't have her address. Although... I do know where she's staying—at the Cotswolds Manor Hotel. I suppose I could ring up and leave a message for her there."

It was mid-afternoon by the time we got back to Oxford and I was itching to get out of my travel-stained clothes, have a hot shower, and just drop into bed. Somehow, although I had slept for much of the flight, I felt exhausted. Maybe it was the jetlag. However, I had barely got into the house when my mother said brightly:

"Now you'll just have time to freshen up, darling, before Mabel and the others get here."

"Who? Mabel who?"

"Mabel Cooke, darling—you remember her! She used to live near us in Meadowford-on-Smythe. In fact, she used to babysit for me when you were very little and we still lived in the village. We had lost touch for a while but I've been seeing much more of her again recently, since I joined the Meadowford Ladies' Society. Anyway, she has been dying to see you so I've invited her over for afternoon tea, together with her friends Glenda Bailey, Florence Doyle, and Ethel Webb. They're lovely—in fact, you might remember Ethel in particular. She used to be the librarian at the village library. She always used to give you a special sticker for returning a book on time... do you remember? They are so excited to see you. And since I was baking anyway, I thought I might as well invite them round for tea."

I groaned inwardly. Yes, I remembered Mabel Cooke: a bossy, formidable woman with a booming voice and a no-nonsense manner. I had been terrified of her as a child—she used to swoop down on me, claiming that I had a spot of dirt on my cheek, then lick her fingers and try to wipe the smudge off with her saliva. *Eeuuww!* Why did parents and older people always do that to children? I used to squirm in revulsion but never dared to say anything or move until she had released me.

Now, tired and jetlagged as I was, the last thing I wanted to do was sit and have afternoon tea with a bunch of old crones who had terrorised me in childhood. Mabel Cooke was probably in her eighties by now—but somehow, I didn't think that she would have mellowed much.

My worst fears were realised when the doorbell rang half an hour later and four little old ladies marched into the house. Mabel was in the lead—I recognised her instantly—and she had hardly changed. Her helmet of woolly hair might have been whiter, perhaps, and her skin more wrinkled around the eyes, but otherwise her voice was as stentorian as ever and her manner just as brisk and bossy.

"Gemma, I'm glad you've finally seen sense, my dear, and come back to England," Mabel said as soon as we all sat down in the living room.

The coffee table was laid out with a full Royal Doulton tea service and a selection of freshly baked scones, hot buttered teacakes, little lemon curd tarts, and home-made shortbread biscuits. My mother was a fantastic baker. I helped myself to a piece of shortbread—beautifully rich and crumbly—

and decided that the delicious baked treats almost made having tea with Mabel and her friends worth it.

My mother poured the tea and handed the cups out, then passed around the plate of scones, still warm from the oven.

"I told your mother a convict colony is no place for a nicely brought-up girl," Mabel said as she cut a scone in half and slathered it heavily with jam and clotted cream.

"Er... Australia isn't a British colony anymore, Mrs Cooke," I said. "And there haven't been convicts sent out there since the 1800s. Sydney is actually a really beautiful, cosmopolitan city—"

"Humph! Don't get cheeky with me, young lady," said Mabel. Then she leaned forwards suddenly, narrowing her eyes. "Is that a spot of dirt on your nose? Here, let me..."

"GAH!" I jerked backwards as Mabel licked her thumb with a big wet tongue and reached out towards me.

"Gemma!" My mother frowned at me.

"Sorry, Mother," I said as I hastily scooted a few inches further down the sofa, away from Mabel Cooke. "I... er... it must be the jetlag."

"Ohhh—I've heard that flying does terrible things to your body," said Glenda Bailey, her pretty wrinkled face screwing up in horror as she balanced a teacup on her knee. "One gets swollen joints and horrible dry skin and even..." she dropped her voice to a delicate whisper, "...*bad breath*!"

"Yes, it is from being up so high and having so little oxygen," said Florence Doyle with a shudder which shook her plump body.

"It's not quite as bad as that," I protested.

"I read a book once when I was still working at the library," said Ethel in her gentle voice. "It was all about the dangers of flying and it said that you were exposed to dreadful radiation from space when you were up in the air—enough to give you cancer several times over! And jetlag is so disruptive that it can lead to heart disease and psychiatric disorders."

Well, thanks very much, I thought. This is exactly what I wanted to hear after I'd been flying for twenty-plus hours, continuously zapped by cosmic rays, and now struggling with jetlag, since it was the middle of the night back in Sydney. I guess all I had to do now was sit back and wait for the cancer and heart disease and psychotic breakdowns—oh, and let's not forget the bad breath—to get me.

"Constipation is the *worst* thing about flying," said Mabel suddenly in her booming voice.

There was a moment of awkward silence as even my mother's usual polite English aplomb failed her. Then she picked up the teapot and said brightly, "More tea, anyone?"

Mabel accepted a fresh cup, then continued, undaunted. "Flying in an airplane gives you gas, bloating, and constipation. But don't worry—I know just the thing. When my Henry and I went on holiday, I made sure to take a bag of prunes with me on the plane. Marvellous things, prunes. Much better than any of those laxatives you can buy at the chemist." She leaned towards me again. "I'll bring some over for you, Gemma—I've got some stewed to a special recipe. Never fear, we'll get your bowels going again!"

I *really* began to wonder if I had made a terrible mistake coming back...

CHAPTER THREE

I looked across the high street of Meadowford-on-Smythe and a broad grin spread across my face as I caught sight of the raven-haired girl on the other side.

"Gemma!" She waved excitedly.

"Cassie!" I hurried across and caught my best friend in a quick hug.

"How was the flight? Was the food awful? Did you get any sleep? Meet any dishy men on the plane?"

I laughed and looked fondly at my pretty, vivacious friend. Cassie never changed. We'd known each other since primary school and had a deep, abiding friendship that had carried us through the hormonal years of high school, the carefree days of university, and even the long separation of my time overseas. And though she was obviously now all grown up—with a killer figure to boot—Cassie was still very much the girl I'd met on the first day of school, searching for ladybirds in the playground. She was still bubbly, warm-hearted, and impulsive— a combo that matched her artistic persona.

Cassie's childhood obsession with painting and drawing had turned into a lifelong dream to be an artist. It was still more dream than reality at the moment (like most artists, Cassie found that, sadly, talent alone didn't pay the bills) and I knew that in order to support her artist lifestyle, she had had to work a selection of part-time jobs—something she hated.

But that was all going to change now, I reminded myself. Cassie was coming to work with *me* and the thought filled me with a rush of happiness.

As if reading my mind, Cassie squeezed my hand and said, "Well? Are you excited?"

"You have no idea," I said. "I can't wait to see it."

She glanced at her watch. "It's nearly six. Come on—we've got a bit of time before the sun goes down. I was hoping we could see it first thing this morning, before I had to go to work, otherwise I knew we'd have to wait until I finished for the day and it's much nicer to see it in daylight—"

"I know... sorry," I said ruefully. "I just couldn't get up this morning. I told myself I'd just sleep a little bit longer—and then the next thing I knew, it was nearly lunchtime! My mother let me sleep, thinking I needed the rest, but I wish she'd forced me to get up."

I shivered and pulled the collar of my duffel coat up higher around my neck. "Brrr... It's really chilly isn't it?"

Cassie chuckled. "You've gone soft, Gemma, since moving out to Australia! This is hardly cold! Wait till you see what it's like in January! It's actually quite warm, I think, for September."

I thrust my hands deeper into my pockets. "Well, you can't blame me—we were heading into summer in Australia when I left and my body's not used to the sudden change. Besides, I forgot about the 'wind chill factor' here." I shivered again as another strong gust of wind blew down the village high street and sliced through the wool of my duffel coat.

"Better get used to it," said Cassie. She made an expression of mock horror and lowered her voice dramatically. "We even have something called 'snow' here—it's this white stuff which is really cold and falls from the sky and you'd better take precautions otherwise it might get you when you least expect it..."

I gave her a playful shove, then we walked slowly through the village, talking and laughing, just as we used to when we were girls. I'd lived in Meadowford until my early teens when my family had moved to North Oxford. Looking around me now, it was as if time had stood still. There was the pub on the corner of the village green, the 14th-century church with its picturesque steeple, and the bustling village high street lined on either side with little shops selling everything from sausages to antiques, knitting wool to vintage books... I suppose it was always like that in these quaint little Cotswolds villages, with their pretty thatched-roof cottages and winding cobbled lanes—like something out of a postcard or a calendar of the English countryside.

At the bottom of the high street was an old Tudor building with an adjoining courtyard. Cassie and I stopped in front of it and I looked up at the historic structure, my heart pounding with excitement. *This* was the reason I had given up everything and come back to England.

It had once been part of a Tudor inn with the adjoining courtyard providing stables for the guests' horses. I remembered it vaguely from my childhood as a shop premises. In more recent times, it had been used as a café. There was a sign, crooked and fading, showing the picture of a coffee cup, and, through the drab lace curtains, we could see some cheap vinyl chairs and laminate tables, as well as a buffet cabinet in that ugly yellow so popular in the 1970s. A few lace doilies were scattered around the tables, together with a few vases of drooping plastic roses.

"It looks a lot worse than I remembered," said Cassie doubtfully, as she peered in the windows. "When I came past last time, before I told you about it on the phone, I didn't think it looked so bad."

"Didn't you say it had been closed for a while?"

"Yeah, for a couple of months, I think. Not that it had that many customers even before it closed," said Cassie wryly. "No one wants to sit in some dark, dingy room to eat stodgy cake and drink lukewarm coffee."

"Well, I'm going to change all that," I said, smiling in anticipation. "It will be completely different when the place is mine. People will come from across Oxfordshire to eat and drink at my tearoom."

Cassie made a face and said, "Gemma—I hate to say this, but are you sure you want to go ahead? You haven't signed anything; the loan hasn't even been approved by the bank yet. You could still change your mind. There are other places, other villages. I'm sure we could find another site and you could always convert it and—"

"No," I said, looking up at the building and admiring the timeless beauty of the "wattle and daub" Tudor exterior with its the dark wood beams and whitewashed walls. Yes, it was in a pretty sorry state and there was a general air of dejection and abandonment about the place. And yet... for the first time since the day I had handed in my notice at my office in Sydney, I felt sure of what I was doing. Gone were the doubts, the panic, and the anxious worrying. It was strange, but standing there, staring at the shabby old café, I knew I was doing the right thing. *You only get one life and I'm going to take the chance to follow a dream.*

"No, I'm not changing my mind," I said to Cassie. "I know this can be beautiful. The building's been standing here for over five hundred years. The bones are all there. We just need to spruce it up and redecorate the inside—strip out that dreadful 70s décor and restore the original period features." I peered in again through the window. "That looks like a real inglenook fireplace, there behind that horrible striped screen. Imagine how gorgeous that's going to look when I turn this back into a traditional English tearoom." I sighed with pleasure at the prospect. "I just need the bank to approve the loan, exchange contracts, get the keys... and then we can get to work!"

"Well, I hope the bank doesn't drag its heels," said Cassie. "I was chatting to the estate agent yesterday and he told me there's been another offer."

"Really? Who? Someone local?"

Cassie shook her head. "No, some giant travel corporation from China that's expanding in the U.K. They want to buy the site and turn it into a gift shop-slash-canteen for their big Chinese tour groups when they come through Oxfordshire."

I looked at Cassie in horror. "But that would be a disaster! They would completely ruin this place! There's so much heritage and history wrapped up in this building—it would be sacrilege to turn this into some tacky gift shop full of cheap plastic keyrings and cheesy Oxford T-shirts!" I shuddered.

"Yeah, everyone in the village agrees with you. They're up in arms about it, but what can you do?" Cassie shrugged helplessly. "They can't really do anything to prevent the sale going through if the owners decide to accept the offer."

"Do you know what the Chinese are offering?"

"More than you are," said Cassie darkly. "But the owners are pretty decent people. They're tired of running this café and they want to move to Spain—but I think they'd like to preserve things as well. They want to try and do the right thing. So I think as long as you can give them what they originally asked for, they'll be content with that. But the Chinese *are* putting pressure on them and it's a tempting offer, so you don't want to delay things." She gave me a wry look. "Not to quote Princess Leia but... you're our only hope, Gemma."

I nodded. "Don't worry—I'll get it. There's no reason why I shouldn't. I've provided everything needed for the application and the bank was very positive. In fact, the chap I spoke to before I left Sydney told me that the loan was practically approved and it was just a formality, getting the official paperwork signed and all that. But everything should be confirmed by the day after tomorrow." A huge yawn overtook me and I had to cover my mouth hurriedly. "Sorry." I gave Cassie a sheepish smile. "I seem to get these waves of tiredness that come over me at odd times."

"It's the jetlag," said Cassie.

"Yeah, it was a really long flight... and when we got back home, Mabel Cooke and her friends came over for tea, so—"

"What? I can't believe you spent the first day back in this country having tea with the Old Biddies!"

"The who?"

"The Old Biddies—that's what I call them. Mabel Cooke and her gang." Cassie grinned. "Not to their faces, of course."

I laughed, then looked up at the tearoom building again in the fading twilight.

"Any idea what you're going to call it?" Cassie asked. "The previous owners were really boring and just called it the Meadowford Café but I was thinking—"

"The Little Stables Tearoom," I said softly, with a smile. "That's what I'm going to call it. And when I'm finished with it, it'll be known for having the best tea and scones in Oxfordshire."

CHAPTER FOUR

"You don't have to rush back for dinner with your parents, do you?" asked Cassie. "We could go to the pub for a drink—and maybe even stay on for dinner. The Blue Boar does really good food in the evenings now."

I smiled. "That sounds great. I haven't had a 'pub meal' in ages. Mmm... I fancy some fish and chips."

"Oh, they do fantastic chips there: thick, chunky, and crispy—and drenched in salt and vinegar... just the way a proper English chip should be. None of that ketchup nonsense!" said Cassie with a laugh.

We walked down to the village pub and I smiled to myself as I stepped into the cosy warmth of the quaint old building, with its low-beamed ceilings and leadlight windows. The Blue Boar was the heart of the village once the sun went down and it was heaving with a mixture of local residents and tourists visiting the Cotswolds region. We wrestled our way through the crowd to the bar and ordered our drinks, then repaired to a snug little wooden booth in the corner. A couple of hours and several drinks later, we ordered some food and I tucked into my first English pub meal with gusto, savouring the soft, flaky white fish coated in crispy beer batter, accompanied by piping hot chips, tangy with salt and malt vinegar. We were just finishing and I was licking the salt from my fingers when my phone rang. I dug it out of my handbag and glanced at the screen. It was a local number I didn't recognise.

"Hello? Gemma Rose speaking."

"Gemma—it's Jenn! Jenn Murray, from the airplane."

"Oh, hi, Jenn—how are you? Did you get my message about your scarf?"

"Yes, I only just got it now actually. There was a bit of a mix-up at the front desk; the hotel seems to be short-staffed and the manager has been off sick— some flu going round—and when the girls on Reception changed shifts, they forgot to pass the message on. Anyway, thanks so much for picking it up for me! I was so upset when I thought I'd lost it— it's my favourite. In fact, I even thought it was stolen from the hotel."

"Stolen?" I said in surprise.

"Yes, there's this maid here—I'm sure she's been going through my things. I caught her with her hands in my handbag this morning, although she pretended to cover it up."

"Have you missed anything?"

"I'm not sure—I think one of my lipsticks is missing; it was a really expensive Christian Dior one and it was brand new. But I suppose I could have forgotten to pack it and left it in Australia..."

"Maybe you ought to report it to the hotel."

"Maybe... although I hate to cause a scene and it's just one lipstick. They'll probably laugh at me. I don't have any proof—but I just have a feeling about this maid. I know you're not supposed to judge on first impressions but there is something about her and the way she looks, all dark-eyed and furtive... and she's bloody nosy too! Kept asking me all these insolent questions the first day I arrived—I mean, are you cleaning my room or doing my family tree? Anyway," Jenn said brightly, "at least I've got my scarf back. Do you think... Would you mind posting it to me?"

"Well actually, I'm quite near your hotel at the moment. I'm in Meadowford-on-Smythe, having dinner with a friend. I could stop off at your hotel on my way home. Lucky for you, the scarf is still in my handbag."

"Oh, could you? That would be wonderful! It's been so cold and windy—it would be fantastic to have my scarf."

I laughed. "I'm glad somebody agrees with me about the cold! Okay, I'll drop it off later..." I glanced at my watch. "I'll probably be there around nine-thirty. See you then!"

***

The Cotswolds Manor Hotel was one of the new breed of resort hotels that were springing up around the English countryside, offering a combination of luxury accommodation, golf facilities, and an in-house spa for bored and neglected wives. It had only opened in the last year or so—I seemed to remember my mother telling me about it in one of our long-distance conversations—and I admired the great job they had done converting the old country manor house into a modern, comfortable hotel.

There was no one on Reception when I arrived in the lobby and I was surprised, especially considering how busy it was. There was a large Japanese tour group congregating in the centre, all chattering away enthusiastically and comparing their Nikon and Canon lenses, whilst scattered throughout the comfortable lounge on the other side of the lobby were several smaller groups of tourists, families, and businessmen.

I remembered Jenn's comment about the hotel being short-staffed and wondered if there was a bell I could ring for attention, but just as I was leaning over the counter to look for it, a tall, suave-looking man stepped out of an inner office behind the reception desk. He saw me and hurried over, his face anxious.

"I'm terribly sorry—have you been waiting long?"

"No, no, I just arrived," I assured him with a smile. "I'd heard that you're a bit short-staffed."

"Yes." He sighed. "It's this flu that's been going round—I'm only just recovering from it myself and this is my first night back—and today, both our receptionists suddenly called in sick at the last moment..." He gave me an apologetic smile. "Anyway, my name is Derek Sutton; I'm the manager. How can I help you?"

"I'm here to see one of your guests." I gave him Jenn's name and room number and he rang her room.

"She's coming right down," he said as he hung up. "Would you like to take a seat in the lounge while you're waiting...?"

He trailed off as his eyes went beyond me and I turned around to find myself facing a tall, handsome man with dark blue eyes and blond hair styled to flop boyishly over his face. He was dressed in a Ralph Lauren blazer coupled with expensive chinos and suede loafers. The designer chic effect was slightly spoiled by one arm being in a sling but that didn't seem to affect his confidence. He had the air of a man who was good-looking and knew it. He was eyeing me with a leer and instantly I felt my hackles go up.

"Hello-hello-hello... Looks like it might be my lucky night," he said, a smile curling the corners of his mouth. "Not checking in, by any chance?"

"No," I said coolly. I was about to turn away again when he thrust his good hand towards me.

"I'm Andrew. And you are... let me see, you look like a Giselle? No, a Selina? Or I know, you must be an Ava?"

"None of those," I said coldly.

He smirked. "Well, go on then, tell me what it is."

I drew back slightly, my English upbringing and the stricture to "always be polite" warring with my desire to tell him to sod off.

Behind me, the hotel manager cleared his throat. "Mr Manning..." he said, his voice heavy with polite disapproval.

Andrew Manning held his good hand up. "All right, all right... But you can't blame a chap for trying when he sees a pretty girl. Anyway—" he winked at me, "—I'll be over there by the bar. Let me know if you'd like a drink... or anything else." He gave me a loaded smile, then sauntered off.

Ugh. I turned away, feeling like I needed a shower. At that moment, there came a soft ping from the lift on the other side of the lobby and, a minute later, Jenn Murray stepped out.

Her eyes lit up and she hurried over. "Gemma! Thank you so much for coming!"

"Oh, no problem—I told you I was in the area," I said, reaching into my handbag and pulling out her scarf. "Here you go."

She took it gratefully. "Thanks so much. I really appreciate you returning it. I have to say, I wasn't prepared for the English weather—I seem to feel cold all the time!" She turned to the manager, who was still standing behind the reception counter. "I was wondering if the hotel supplied hot water bottles? I know you probably think that's a bit pathetic but I'm dreading the thought of getting into bed tonight."

Derek Sutton looked taken aback and stared at her for a moment, then quickly recovered his poise and said smoothly, "Not at all, madam. We understand our guests come from all over the world and may be used to different climates. I will check with Room Service and see if they can locate a hot water bottle to send to your room."

He turned away to speak on the internal phone and Jenn turned back to me.

"He probably thinks I'm mad," she said in an undertone, laughing.

"I'm sure they're pretty used to dealing with guests' eccentricities." I smiled at her. "Anyway, I'll head off now. I hope you enjoy the rest of your stay and—"

"Oh, wait—don't go," said Jenn. She gave me a shy smile. "Do you... Would you like a drink? I don't think I'll be able to sleep for hours yet and I don't really fancy going back to sit alone in my room..."

I hesitated. It was a quarter to ten and I should probably have been getting back. On the other hand, it wasn't as if there was anything to rush back for. My parents were early sleepers and would probably be in bed by now, which meant that I would have to tiptoe around the house. I didn't fancy going back to sit alone in my room either and, with the jetlag, I'd probably be wide-awake for several hours yet.

I accepted her invitation and we headed over to the lounge area, settling into seats near the bar. The bartender came to take our orders and Jenn looked at me in surprise as I ordered a glass of lemonade.

"You're not driving, are you?" she said.

"Oh, no, I'm getting a taxi back. But I'm not much of a drinker, to be honest. I've had a couple of drinks earlier this evening already."

"Well, then I'll just have to drink for both of us," said Jenn with a grin as she gave the order for a double vodka martini.

As we waited for our drinks, a man sitting at a table across from us leaned over and gave us a knowing wink, followed by a jaunty wave. It was Andrew Manning.

"Oh God, not him again," muttered Jenn.

"I've had a run-in with him too," I admitted. "Loves himself a bit, doesn't he?"

"He's an absolute creep," said Jenn. "And I've got the misfortune to be in the room next to him. He kept trying to chat me up earlier this evening when we happened to be in the lift together. I thought I'd shut him up by telling him I was too old for him, but he had the cheek to say that he preferred older women!"

I laughed and shook my head. "Some people are just so thick-skinned."

"The good-looking ones are the worst, I think,"

said Jenn. "They've probably been used to girls falling over them since high school and they think they're God's gift to women."

I laughed again. "Yeah, now that you mention it, I remember this boy at university who was very handsome and everyone used to say he looked like Tom Cruise. Bloody hell, did he milk it! In fact, I think he even got some modelling work as a lookalike…"

"Mm… I actually think a lot of people look like celebrities. Like that guy sitting across from us on the plane. Didn't you think he looked a bit like George Clooney?"

I did an exaggerated stare. "Are you sure? I think I would have noticed if someone looked like George Clooney!"

Jenn chuckled. "Maybe it was just the dim light in the cabin, then. Okay, what about the hotel manager? He reminds me of someone—"

"Robert Redford?" I suggested. "He's got that dark blond hair and the square-jawed good looks."

"Hmm, maybe…" She didn't look convinced. "Oh, I've just realised that *you* remind me of someone too!"

"Me? Who?"

"Audrey Hepburn. You've got the same petite frame and big dark eyes and the short hair in a pixie bob…"

"Really?" I beamed, rather flattered. "Thanks."

The bartender returned with our drinks and we settled back in our seats. I found myself telling Jenn all about the tearoom. She was a good listener and, in a way, it was nice talking to a stranger about it—someone who didn't know me and didn't have any expectations. We discussed the renovations I was going to do and even had fun thinking up some items for the menu.

"I think it's wonderful what you're doing," said Jenn enthusiastically. "It takes a lot of courage to give up a cushy job and take a risk like that, but I think you're doing the right thing."

"I hope so," I said. "Otherwise, it's going to be a very expensive mistake!" I glanced at my watch and was surprised to see that it was nearly ten-thirty already. Jenn was on her fourth martini and she was about to signal the bartender for another refill.

"Are you sure you should be having another one?" I blurted out. "Sorry, I just thought..." I stammered, embarrassed, cursing my wayward tongue. It was really none of my business if Jenn wanted to drink until she was unconscious under the table.

Jenn giggled. "Don't worry, I can hold my drink," she said, slurring her words slightly. She hesitated, then waved the bartender away. "But maybe you're right and I'd better stop."

"And I'd better head for home now," I said, rising.

"I'll come and see you off," said Jenn. She stood up, swaying slightly, and as she tried to push her chair back, she lost her balance and nearly fell over.

"Oops!" She giggled again. "Maybe I *have* had a bit too much..."

"Maybe I should come up with you to your room," I said in concern.

"Eh? No—no need! I'll be fine!" she insisted as she stepped away from the table and began trying to cross the lounge. She tripped and lurched sideways, nearly toppling into a potted palm by the wall.

I caught her elbow to steady her. "Whoa! Okay, come on, I'm seeing you up to your room," I said, not giving her any more chance to argue.

CHAPTER FIVE

I steered Jenn towards the lift and stood waiting impatiently for it to arrive, with Jenn sagging heavily onto my right shoulder. For a modern hotel, they certainly hadn't planned things very well. There was only one lift and while it was beautiful, in an antique style with an ornate metal cage exterior, it seemed to be working at a 17th-century speed.

Finally, it arrived and I shepherded my new friend into the compartment and then up to the third floor. Outside her door, I propped her against the wall whilst I prised the key from her hands. This door, like the lift, was done in an antique style, with an old-fashioned lock to match, and I had to jiggle it a few times before it opened. At last, I escorted Jenn in and deposited her on the bed, then went into the bathroom and drew a glass of cold water.

"Here," I said, thrusting it at her. "Drink this. You need to get some water into you."

She took it obediently and finished the glass. Perhaps the cold water revived her, because her eyes looked slightly less glazed as she put the glass down on the bedside table.

"Thanks for that, Gemma," she said, giving a little hiccup. "I'm sorry... That was a bit embarrassing... I don't know why I let myself drink that much..."

"Well, you can sleep it off now," I said kindly. "Is there anything else you need?"

"No, I think I'm..." She looked around and gave a gasp. "Where's my handbag?"

"Your handbag? Don't you have it? I saw you picking it up when we left the table—"

"I did and I was holding it... But I don't have it now..." She looked around wildly. "I must have dropped it on our way up!"

I sighed. "Don't worry, I'll pop down and get it. It's probably still in the lounge—or maybe on the lobby floor somewhere. You just wait here."

I left the room and paused for a moment. There was a back staircase right by Jenn's room, whereas the lift was down the other end of the long corridor, but I decided to be lazy and use the lift. Soon I was regretting this decision because it seemed to take the lift ages to arrive again. Just as I was deciding that I might brave the stairs after all, it pinged softly and the doors opened. I started to step in, then jerked back, embarrassed. There was a couple already in there, locked in a passionate kiss.

"Oh! Excuse me!" I cried, my face flaming as I saw the way they were groping each other.

They didn't seem to hear me and I hovered uncertainly. The last thing I wanted to do was ride down in a small, confined space next to them! As I stood there, undecided, the doors slid shut again and the lift continued down without me. I sighed. *Why can't people just get a room?* I thought irritably, jabbing my finger on the call button again.

There was another long wait before the lift returned, this time thankfully empty of amorous couples. A few minutes later, I was back in the lobby, my eyes scanning the floor for any sign of a fallen handbag. I walked down the length of the lobby, trying to retrace our route, then wandered into the lounge area. There was now a large group of German tourists occupying most of the seats, talking and laughing boisterously. They had moved some of the tables and chairs around in order to sit together and it completely disorientated me. I couldn't remember which table we had been sitting at.

It took several more minutes of frustrated searching before I finally spotted the handbag, tucked underneath an armchair. Relieved, I grabbed it and headed back to the lift, for another torturous wait before the doors finally opened and a group of giggling women spilled out. I took their place in the lift car, wrinkling my nose against the cloying perfume they had left in their wake, and ascended once more to the third floor.

Just as I was about to step out, I almost collided with someone rushing in. His shoulder smacked into mine, making me stagger backwards.

"Oh!" I gasped, surprised and annoyed.

It was Andrew Manning, I realised, though he didn't look anything like his earlier smug self. He was breathing rapidly, his face pale and sweaty. I wondered if he had had a nasty put-down by some woman he had been trying to chat up and couldn't help feeling a malicious stab of pleasure at the thought. It was time someone took him down a peg or two!

The lift doors shut behind me and I hurried back to Jenn's room. The door was slightly ajar—had I not pulled it shut properly when I left? Possibly I did, but the stiff lock hadn't latched properly.

"Jenn? It's Gemma." I knocked and pushed the door open.

There was no one in the room but I could hear Jenn in the bathroom, using an electric toothbrush. I smiled, glad that she was getting ready for bed properly. I'd gone to bed a few times without taking my make-up off or brushing my teeth, and it was horrible waking up in the morning!

"I found your handbag," I called. "It had fallen under one of the armchairs in the lounge. I'll just leave it here on the table by the door."

"Thank you...!" came the garbled reply, as the buzz of the electric toothbrush was followed by the whooshing of water in the sink.

"Good night! Sleep well."

I withdrew my head and pulled the door firmly shut, then took one final trip down in the lift. The lobby was still as busy and noisy as ever, although the reception counter was empty again. I heaved an impatient sigh—I'd been hoping the hotel could call a taxi for me. I wandered over to the main entrance, hoping that I might be able to snag a taxi from an arriving guest, although I didn't think there would be many people arriving this late at night now. And from what I could see through the sliding glass doors, it looked like it had started raining. Still, it was better than standing around in here. As I was about to step out into the cold, however, a side door next to the entrance opened and Derek Sutton, the hotel manager, stepped in. He was wearing a coat and his hair was slightly ruffled.

"Brr!" he said, giving me a smile and rubbing his hands. "I think your Australian friend was right after all. It's a chilly night out there..."

I must have looked curious because he smiled ruefully and explained, "It's the curse of being a smoker. Now that we're no longer allowed to light up indoors, we have to brave the elements every time we want our nicotine fix." He looked at me more closely. "You're not staying at the hotel, are you? Forgive me, I've only come back on duty today and I'm not that familiar with the new guests yet."

"No, I'm not. I'm just leaving actually, and I was

hoping to order a taxi."

"Oh, they should be able to order one for you at …" He trailed off as his gaze went to the empty reception counter. He frowned. "Where's that girl got to? I've asked one of the maids to help out on Reception as she's had some experience on a front desk and she wasn't supposed to leave it unattended…" He sighed, then gave me an anxious smile. "I'm very sorry about the service this evening. I hope you'll believe me when I say that this isn't the norm for the Cotswolds Manor Hotel."

"No, of course not," I murmured politely.

"I'll personally order the taxi for you—and the hotel will pay the fare, as a gesture of apology," said Derek Sutton quickly.

"Oh, that's very kind of you but it's really not necessary—"

"I insist. If you'll come with me and give me the address…"

The side door suddenly opened again and a young woman in a maid's uniform burst out, breathing rapidly, as if she had been running. She had a Mediterranean look about her, with black hair and olive skin and flashing dark eyes. She stopped short when she saw us.

"Marie! Where have you been? I thought I'd asked you to stay on Reception?" said Derek Sutton in the tight tone that people use when they're very angry but trying to remain polite in public.

"I'm sorry, sir, but a guest needed something

upstairs..." She trailed off. I realised that the side door led into a stairwell which connected with the staircase that led up to all the floors, as well as providing access to the outside.

"Please remain on Reception until the end of your shift," said Derek Sutton icily. "If there is anything that needs attention upstairs, please ask one of the other maids or myself."

"Yes, sir," she said sullenly, following us back to the reception counter.

The hotel manager ordered my taxi himself and then, after plying me with more apologies, finally disappeared back into his office. As I waited for the taxi to arrive, I glanced across the lobby lounge and saw Andrew Manning standing alone at the bar. He was downing a large whiskey and still looked very shaken. I smiled to myself and wondered what kind of dressing down he had received to leave him so rattled. Good for that woman. I almost wished I had been a fly on the wall!

***

I was roused from the depths of sleep the next morning by my mother's voice calling through my door.

"Mm-mmph...?" I raised my head off the pillow, looking blearily around. From the light shining in through a gap in the curtains, it must have been mid-morning already. I sighed. I had been meaning to get up earlier to get my body clock back on track but it looked like I had overslept again.

Then I realised my mother was still calling me through the door. "Gemma? Darling, are you awake?" She knocked and opened the door. "There's someone on the phone for you."

"Who?" I said, yawning and rubbing my eyes.

"The police."

"The police?" I stared at her in surprise. "Why?"

"I don't know, darling—something about an accident at the Cotswolds Manor Hotel."

Frowning, I got out of bed, pulled on my dressing gown, and followed my mother downstairs.

I picked up the phone in the hall. "Hullo?"

"Miss Gemma Rose? This is Inspector Glenn of the Oxfordshire CID. I understand that you're a friend of Jenn Murray's?"

"Yes, that's right—well, I only met her recently on the plane, coming back from Australia, but I suppose you could say we're friends."

"And you had drinks with her last night at the hotel?"

"Yes, that's right," I said again. "Why? What's happened?"

"Can you tell me what time you left her?"

"I think it must have been just after 11 p.m. Why? What's going on? And how did you get my number?"

"We contacted the taxi company. They gave us the address you were dropped off at and we traced the number accordingly."

"But why did you need to trace me? I don't understand—"

"Miss Rose, I'm afraid I have some bad news for you. Your friend, Jenn Murray, is dead."

"*Dead?* What do you mean—dead? How?" I leaned against the hall table, shocked.

"A maid went into her room this morning and found her collapsed in the bathroom. She had suffered a blow to the head."

"But... but she was fine when I left. I mean, she was a bit drunk but I thought she would just sleep it off. Oh God, maybe I shouldn't have left her... Did she have an accident?"

There was a moment's hesitation, then the inspector said, "We are conducting an investigation and we'd like you to answer some questions. I'm currently at the hotel, interviewing some of the staff and other guests. If you could come here, it would save me having to return to the station. I could get my sergeant to come and pick you up."

"Yes, of course, that's fine but... I don't understand—what do you mean, conducting an investigation? Didn't Jenn just fall down and hit her head in the bathroom?"

The inspector's voice was carefully neutral. "There is some uncertainty over the cause of death. The blow to her head was not accidental."

I caught my breath. "You don't mean... Jenn was murdered?"

CHAPTER SIX

I stood and looked around the empty hotel room, noting the open suitcase in the corner, and the laptop on the desk with various papers and the Oxford tour guide next to it. The bright blue turquoise scarf hung over the back of a chair and I swallowed convulsively. I couldn't believe that Jenn was dead.

I almost couldn't nerve myself to go into the bathroom, even though I knew they had already removed the body. I followed the inspector silently as he led me through the adjoining door and glanced over the vanity counter—the little group of creams and lotions, the quilted gold cosmetic bag, the wooden hairbrush and a couple of elastic hair ties, the electric toothbrush standing forlornly by itself next to the sink... I swallowed again and turned hastily away.

"Does everything look the same as last night?" asked Inspector Glenn, a grizzled detective in his mid-sixties, with a balding head and shrewd brown eyes beneath bushy grey eyebrows. He reminded me slightly of a large terrier and seemed to share the same suspicious nature and aggressive tenacity.

I skimmed the rest of the bathroom, taking in the toilet, shower, and bathtub, the towels hanging on the rails, the little bottles of shampoo and conditioner, then gave a helpless shrug.

"I suppose so. To be honest with you, I wasn't paying that much attention. I was only in the room briefly—I helped Jenn to the bed and then came in here to get a glass of water for her to drink." I looked at him. "Are you thinking that someone came in here after me and moved things around?"

"No one has been in the room since the body was discovered by the maid this morning," said Inspector Glenn. "She called the police immediately and we were lucky that a patrol was in the neighbourhood so they arrived and secured the scene. There's been a constable on guard at the door ever since." He leaned forwards and looked at me intently. "You seem to be the last person to have seen Jenn Murray alive— which means that any change you notice now may be a clue to the murderer."

I winced at the word. "I'm sorry—I really can't be sure if something specific has changed." I wandered back into the bedroom and scanned the room. "It all looks pretty much the same to me—the suitcase was in the corner over there, and her scarf draped over the chair... and I think that laptop and those papers were on the desk like that..." I turned my head. "And her handbag is still there, where I left it." I looked at the inspector. "Was her wallet stolen? Her jewellery? Money?"

"No, nothing was taken." He gestured to the handbag. "What was that you said about the bag being where you left it?"

I recounted what had happened the night before, explaining how I had helped Jenn up to her room and then my second trip downstairs and back to retrieve her handbag.

"What time did you bring Ms Murray up to her room?"

"I don't know—I think it must have been just after ten-thirty."

"And you left immediately again to return downstairs for the handbag?"

"Yes, pretty much—I only stayed a few minutes to get her a glass of water."

"I've questioned the bartender and a few of the guests who were in the lounge last night. They did remember seeing you search for a handbag but they said it was closer to eleven o'clock."

I shrugged, not sure what he was getting at. "Yeah, probably—I wasn't really watching the time. But what does it matter? Jenn wasn't found until this morning—she could have been killed anytime in the night or even the early hours?"

"The pathologist has put the time of death at sometime between nine-thirty and eleven-thirty. Since Ms Murray was seen down in the lobby until around half past ten, she must have been killed in the hour after she went up to her room." He paused, then added in a carefully neutral voice, "One of the German guests was standing in the lobby by the lift and he remembered getting a call just as you walked past him. The phone register shows that his call came in at 10:51 p.m."

"So?" I said, puzzled and starting to feel impatient at these pedantic statements.

"So... it seems strange that you claim to have left Ms Murray's room around ten-forty and yet it took you over ten minutes to arrive downstairs?" The inspector raised his eyebrows. I didn't like the tone of his voice.

"Well, the lift was really slow," I said, trying not to sound defensive. "And when one finally came, there was a couple in it."

"A couple?"

"Yes, you know... they were... um... kissing... and stuff." I flushed slightly. "I didn't really want to ride down in the same lift with them so I decided to wait for the next one. So it took me quite a while before I got back down to the lobby."

"I see." Again, I didn't like his tone. "And then you found Ms Murray's handbag and went straight back upstairs?"

"Yes, as soon as I could get the lift," I said tartly.

"I went back to her room and returned her handbag."

"What time was that?"

"I think it was just after eleven o'clock."

"And did Ms Murray seem all right to you?"

"Yes, she was in the bathroom. I came downstairs, got a taxi, and went home."

"Yes, we've already questioned Mr Sutton, the manager. He went off duty shortly after you left but he confirms that he ordered your taxi and saw you leave, before he left the hotel himself."

"Well, of course, he saw me leave," I said sharply. "Why wouldn't he?"

Inspector Glenn said nothing for a moment. Then he asked, "You said you met Ms Murray on the flight over from Australia?"

"Yes," I said evenly. "We had seats next to each other."

"Got very friendly, didn't you?"

"We were sitting next to each other on a twenty-hour flight—it was only natural to start chatting."

"What did you talk about?"

I shrugged. "All sorts of things... Flying—she was a really nervous passenger—and holidays and coming back to the U.K.... I guess we felt an instant bond because we were both British expats living in Australia. I mean, her accent was pretty Aussie but I'm fairly certain she was originally English."

"And did Ms Murray mention the reason for her trip?"

I frowned. "No, not really. I got the impression that

she was visiting on holiday. She said she got a good package deal at the hotel here—and she had that tour guide with her." I nodded towards the book on Oxford sitting on the desk.

"Why Oxford?"

"I don't know. It's a popular tourist destination, isn't it? Jenn seemed quite private and I didn't like to pry." I hesitated. "She did seem very familiar with the University... and I think she mentioned coming to Oxford as a child or something."

"And so you met on the plane, had a bit of a chat, and then you came to spend the evening with her?" The inspector raised his eyebrows again. "Are you always so chummy with strangers?"

"Well, it wasn't a social call initially. Jenn had left a scarf on the plane and I picked it up. I happened to be in Meadowford village nearby, so when she got in touch, I said I'd drop it off at the hotel. She invited me to stay and have a drink with her and I accepted."

"A drink? That's it?"

"Well, it turned into a couple of drinks—" I broke off and frowned at him. "What are you insinuating?"

The Inspector gave me a patronising smile. "Oh, come now, Miss Rose—there's no need to be coy with me. I'm a man of the world. If your friendship with Ms Murray was a bit more—shall we say, *intimate* in nature—you don't need to conceal it from me."

"What?" I stared at him incredulously. "No, of course we weren't '*intimate*'! Where on earth did you get that idea from?"

He shrugged. "I have my sources. And..." He leaned forwards. "I've done some checking up on you. You were living in Darlinghurst, a well-known gay suburb in Sydney."

I rolled my eyes. "Yes, but there are straight people living in Darlinghurst as well! It happens to be one of the trendiest suburbs in central Sydney. Lots of young people like to live there. It's a short walk to the shopping malls in the city, it's near Hyde Park and public transport, and there are loads of great cafés and eateries."

"So you deny that there was any relationship of a sexual nature between you and Ms Murray?"

"Of course I deny it! It's a ridiculous assumption! Why can't two women just meet and become friends?" I stopped suddenly as the realisation dawned on me. "Am I a suspect? Do you think I murdered Jenn?"

"You were the last person to see her alive," said the inspector.

"But... that's... that's crazy! Why on earth would I want to murder Jenn?" I paused, then said urgently, "I just remembered. There was a man—his name is Andrew Manning and he has the room next to Jenn's—he was harassing her earlier in the evening, trying to chat her up, and she rebuffed him. I passed him as I was stepping out of the lift when I returned upstairs with Jenn's handbag."

"When was this?"

"I told you, around eleven o'clock. He got in the lift

just as I was getting out. He looked really agitated, like breathing really fast, and he was very pale. I saw him again downstairs later—he was having a drink at the bar and still looked very shaken. I remember thinking that he must have had a nasty telling-off by some woman he had tried to chat up. Maybe it was Jenn! Maybe he had gone to her room and they had had an argument or something—and he was smarting from her comments. Some men can't bear to be rejected, can they? And he looks like the type who has a huge ego. Maybe he finished his drink, went back up and... and killed her." I leaned forwards. "You should be questioning him!"

"We will be questioning everyone in connection with the case," said the inspector pompously. "You need not concern yourself with that. And now, if you'll follow my sergeant downstairs, he'll type up your statement and you can read it and sign it." He indicated the young man who had been scribbling notes next to us. "I will be speaking to you again, Miss Rose, and I would advise you not to leave Oxford for the time being. If you do, you must advise the police of your intended destination."

With these ominous parting words, he escorted me to the door.

CHAPTER SEVEN

I tried to hold my head high as I walked past the inspector and yanked the door open. A young woman in the doorway fell forwards, stumbling sideways to avoid crashing into me.

"Oh!" she cried, flushing.

She was wearing a maid's uniform and I recognised her as Marie, the girl whom I had seen behind the reception counter last night. From the way she had fallen into the room, she must have been leaning against the door. Had she been eavesdropping on the interview?

She straightened up and re-arranged her clothing, giving me an accusing look. "I was just about to knock—you opened the door so quickly, you startled me." Her gaze went beyond me to Inspector Glenn and she said, "I... I was just wondering if the room needs to be cleaned, sir?"

"Hmm?" He glanced up from some papers he was examining by the desk. "No, no... this room is off limits. It's a crime scene, and until I release it, no one is to enter without permission."

"Yes, sir." Marie bowed her head, then with another dark look at me, she turned and slipped out of the room.

I followed her and was just in time to see the door to the back staircase swing shut. The sergeant turned the other way and began walking down the long, L-shaped corridor to the lift at the other end. I threw one last look over my shoulder, then followed him. When we arrived downstairs, I was led into the inner office behind the reception counter. It looked like Derek Sutton had been kicked out of his manager's office—the police had appropriated it as a temporary Incident Room while they conducted interviews at the hotel. A constable was sitting behind the desk but he stood up hurriedly when he saw us.

I waited restlessly while the sergeant typed up my statement, then signed it and left the office with some relief. As I was crossing the lobby, I saw Marie the maid again. She was standing in a corner of the lounge, deep in conversation with a young man with slicked-back hair and a black leather jacket. Her eyes lit up when she saw me and she pointed quickly towards me. The young man detached himself from her and sauntered over in my direction.

"Miss Gemma Rose?" he said, giving me an ingratiating smile.

"How do you know my name?"

His smile widened. "It's my business to know things." He stuck a hand out. "My name's Brett. Brett Lyle. I'm a reporter with the *Cotswolds Post*. I was wondering if I could ask you a few questions about the murder? I understand you were the last person to see the victim alive?"

"I have nothing to say," I said, trying to brush past him.

"Aww—don't be like that!" He put a hand out to stop me. "It's only a few questions." He leaned forwards and lowered his voice suggestively. "My paper pays well for exclusives—I'd make it worth your while..."

"No thanks. I'm not interested." I turned away.

"I would have thought that you'd want to set the record straight," he said slyly.

I stopped and turned back to him. "What do you mean?"

"Well... Tongues are wagging, you know... small village like this... there's a lot of gossip. Everyone is wondering about your... *friendship*... with the victim." He put a slight emphasis on the word "friendship" which somehow made it sound dirty.

I thought suddenly of Inspector Glenn's insinuations and flushed angrily. "Is this ridiculous rumour about Jenn and me being lovers?"

His face lit up with glee. "So you admit it!"

"I'm not admitting anything! I just told you—it's a ridiculous rumour! We only met on the plane—"

"Oh! So it was a whirlwind romance!"

"What? No! Stop twisting what I'm saying!" I cried angrily. "We just happened to sit next to each other on a long flight and we got chatting—that's all! Why can't two women be friends these days without all sorts of lewd assumptions being made?"

"I quite agree, I quite agree," said the young reporter, nodding sympathetically. "That's why I thought you'd like the chance to tell your story. Set the record straight. So everyone doesn't think you murdered your lover in a jealous fit—"

"What?" I spluttered "That's—that's so ludicrous, it doesn't even bear answering!"

"So are you saying that you *didn't* murder Jenn Murray out of jealousy?" he said quickly.

"Of course I didn't murder her out of jealousy—I mean—I didn't murder her at all!" I said, furious at the way he was befuddling me and putting words in my mouth. "I'm not talking to you anymore about this!"

I rushed out of the hotel. Outside, I was relieved to find a taxi pulling up to deposit a guest and I barely gave the poor man time to pay his fare before I elbowed him out of the way and climbed in.

I really must dig out my old bicycle and pump up the tyres, I thought as the taxi pulled away from the hotel. I didn't have a car and it was a nightmare having to rely on public transport, especially in these out-of-the-way country places. And taking taxis everywhere was getting expensive.

When I got home, I made good my word by taking myself off to the shed at the back of my parents' garden and searching through the accumulated junk.

Ten minutes later, my mother popped her head in. "Whatever are you doing, darling?" she asked.

"Looking for my bike," I said, as I stepped over a large bag of fertiliser and lifted a couple of tins of paint out of my way.

"Oh, that old thing. We got rid of it a few years ago," said my mother.

I stared at her in dismay. "You got rid of my bike?"

"Yes, it was taking up so much room and you know neither your father nor I cycle. There was a charity auction going on at the church fête and they were looking for donations. I didn't think you'd be back from Sydney anytime soon, so I decided I might as well donate your bicycle."

"But Mother—that was a top-of-the-range Cannondale road bike!" I said, irritated.

"Yes, and it fetched a very good price at auction. All the proceeds went to Save the Bolivian Sloth," said my mother proudly.

"Save the *what*?" I sighed and resisted the urge to grind my teeth.

There was nothing for it but to get myself a new bicycle. *I'll go to Penny Farthing*, I decided. It was the best bike shop in Oxford and it was where I had bought my first bicycle. It would also give me a chance to pop into the city centre and have a look around.

One of the biggest downsides of moving to Australia had been how expensive it was to come back to this side of the world. You could never pop back for a weekend—just the flight alone would take a day, not to mention the horrendous jetlag on either side. And my high-powered executive job hadn't left me with much time for holidays. So what with all that and the ridiculous price of long-distance plane tickets, I hadn't come back home as often as I would have liked. The last time I had been back in England was about three years ago. I doubted that Oxford itself would have changed much—it was one of those timeless, historic cities—but it would be nice to revisit some of my old haunts and take a trip down Memory Lane. At the very least, it would take my mind off the subject of Jenn's murder...

him in years. The sharpness of the memory took me by surprise. Maybe it was coming back home to Oxford and all the old, familiar surroundings...

I pushed the memories away and concentrated determinedly on the future instead. *Tomorrow I should be getting the bank approval on the loan and signing the final papers!* I felt that thrill of anticipation again as I imagined myself picking up the keys to my new tearoom. The thought spurred me on. I finished my lunch quickly, then left The Nosebag and headed down the lane to where the bike shop was located. A few minutes later, I was surveying a row of gleaming bicycles.

"This is the latest range of hybrid bikes," said the shop assistant, running a proud hand over the handlebars of the bicycle next to me. "They combine the speed and agility of a road bike with the power and robustness of a mountain bike, as well as boasting stylish looks for an urban environment... Or if you're the more rugged, outdoor sort, there's the adventure bikes and proper mountain bikes—all-terrain, trail-blazer tyres, travel suspension fork, hydro discs, six-speed Shimano transmission... Or if you're just wanting something for biking around town, these commuter bikes offer the perfect blend of speed, comfort, and practicality—they've got wide-ratio gearing, ergonomic triple-density grips..."

His voice faded into the distance, the technical words bouncing off my ears, as my eyes strayed from the gleaming row of sleek black monsters in front of me to a little blue bicycle in the far corner of the shop.

"What about that one?" I interrupted him.

He stopped in mid-flow and gaped at me. "That one? But that's... that's an old bike that a student brought in yesterday. She was leaving Oxford so she sold it back to us. But that's a second-hand trade-in, a very basic bicycle. It hasn't got multi-gear transmission or the latest suspension styles—it even relies on old-fashioned coaster brakes. Really, it's the kind of thing that... *ahem*... a lady of a certain senior age might ride."

I walked slowly over to examine the old bicycle. It was a baby blue with cream tires, old-fashioned curved handlebars, a slightly rusty metal bell, and a wire basket at the front. It looked quaint and faded and well past its prime. Certainly not the kind of thing I should have been buying to whizz around town in. And yet... something about this creaky old bicycle called to me.

"You'll hardly be able to get up any speed in that old thing," said the shop assistant with a disdainful look.

Well, what was the rush anyway? I thought. I'd been running as fast as I could for eight years in the corporate rat race but I'd jumped off that ship now. My old hectic life was behind me and my new life was going to be different. And surely this little bicycle was much more suitable for the owner of a Cotswolds village tearoom?

"I'll take this one," I said suddenly.

The shop assistant stared. "Are you sure? I must remind you that it *is* second-hand. We service all of our bikes before sale, of course, but an older bike is more likely to develop issues. I can't guarantee—"

"That's okay." I smiled at him. "I'll take my chances."

Resigned, he detached the bicycle and wheeled it over to the cash desk for me. "Are you a student at the University?" he asked. "We're doing a special discount for students at the moment."

"No," I said, flattered to think that I still looked young enough to pass. Then I realised that with the number of graduates coming to Oxford, it probably wasn't a compliment on my youthful looks! "I did used to be a student here—and actually, I bought my first bike from you ages ago. I don't suppose my old university card would still work?" I asked jokingly.

He grinned. "We'll see what we can do. We like to keep our old regulars happy."

A little while later, I walked out of the store, proudly wheeling my new bicycle. As I turned onto the main street leading north out of Oxford, I wondered if it was true that you never forgot how to ride a bike. I hadn't been on one in eight years—I'd meant to get one when I moved to Sydney, but somehow never got around to it.

Slowly, I mounted the bicycle and put my foot experimentally on the pedals, then I pushed off, wobbling down the street. My confidence grew as the bicycle gathered speed and I didn't fall off the seat or crash into the curb. *It's true—you don't forget!* I felt a silly grin of elation spread over my face. Then I was seized by an urge to show off my achievement.

I'll go and see Cassie, I decided. Besides, I wanted to tell her about Jenn's murder. I glanced at the time. It was late afternoon now and I knew she would be teaching a class at the dance studio in Meadowford-on-Smythe. Cassie came from a family of artists and dancers, and she had learned ballet almost before she could walk—a skill that came in very handy when she needed some part-time gigs to supplement her income.

Pumping the pedals with fresh enthusiasm, I headed eagerly out of Oxford.

CHAPTER NINE

I cycled slowly to Meadowford and arrived slightly out of breath but with my cheeks flushed from the fresh air and exercise. I got to the studio and was pleased to catch Cassie just as she was arriving too.

"I see you've been busy," she observed with a grin as I dismounted.

"More than you think," I retorted and told her about the police interview that morning.

"Bloody hell!" said Cassie when I'd finished. "So you think this Andrew Manning chap did it?"

"I wouldn't be surprised," I said grimly. "The man was a creep."

"The detective inspector sounds like a right plonker as well," Cassie commented. "I can't believe he actually suggested that you might be a suspect!"

I gave a dismissive wave. "I don't think he

seriously meant it—I think he was just 'fishing'—besides, that was before I told him about Andrew Manning."

"Yeah, that was rotten luck for Manning being seen by you," said Cassie. "I'll bet he would have lied to the police about his movements last night, otherwise."

I nodded. "Oh, for sure! But I don't think he can wriggle out of it now. Besides, there will probably be forensic evidence as well. I wonder when the police will make the formal arrest?" I frowned. "And I suppose there will be an inquest as well. Inspector Glenn didn't mention it but I assume I'll have to give evidence..."

"What a way to start your new life back in England, huh?" said Cassie with a grim smile. "Witness in a murder enquiry!"

"Well, it can only get better after this," I said wryly as I chained my new bike to a post on the street and followed her into the studio.

The woman behind the reception looked up and said, "Oh, Cassie, I'm afraid you'll have to use Studio 2 for your class today. One of the mirrors in Studio 1 is cracked. Fletcher's in there now replacing it."

"Oh, Fletcher's here? Good, I wanted you to meet him," said Cassie, grabbing my arm and dragging me after her into the adjoining room.

"Who's Fletcher?" I said, following her in puzzlement.

"He's sort of the unofficial handyman in the

village—does a few odd jobs here and there, a bit of gardening and maintenance. But the reason I wanted you to meet him is because he's a fantastic baker. Seriously, his cakes and scones are out of this world."

Inside the studio room, a large man with slightly stooped shoulders and a receding hairline was crouched by the wall of mirrors at the other end. He looked up as we entered. I gave him a smile but he looked quickly away.

"Fletcher's very shy," said Cassie in an undertone. "And he doesn't say much. He's a bit... um... *different*. But don't worry, you get used to it."

"Hey, Fletcher," she said aloud, going across the room to him. "This is my friend, Gemma. Remember I told you about her? She's been living in Australia."

The big man nodded. "With the kangaroos," he said with childlike simplicity.

"Yeah, with the kangaroos," Cassie agreed, giving me a wink behind his back. "Well, she's come back to England now! And guess what? She's going to open a tearoom in the village." She stopped and sniffed the air appreciatively. "Mmm, Fletcher, smells like you've been baking again! What have you made this time?"

The handyman nodded towards a canvas tool bag nearby. Propped against it was a brown paper bag. "I made some scones for everybody," he said.

Cassie's eyes lit up. She pounced on the paper bag and pulled out a scone, which she thrust into my hands. "Here! You have to try one."

Before I could answer, she was already pulling out a second scone and cramming it into her mouth.

"Mmm... so good..." Cassie said, her mouth full. She looked at Fletcher. "Don't suppose you've got any jam or clotted cream with you?"

Fletcher shook his head, looking slightly distressed. "No, Barb did not ask for any jam or cream," he said, referring to the receptionist. "She only asked for scones. A dozen scones, she said. So I made thirteen. A baker's dozen. She did not tell me to bring jam or cream."

"I was only joking, Fletcher," said Cassie, chuckling. "I wouldn't have expected you to have a whole English afternoon tea set-up in your tool bag! These are delicious on their own anyway."

I took a bite of my own scone, then my eyes widened. Cassie was right—it was absolutely delicious: light and fluffy, with a golden crust on the outside and a rich buttery taste. I swallowed, then took another bite and another and another, and before I knew it, all I had left were a few crumbs in my hands. I had to restrain myself from reaching into the paper bag for another scone.

Cassie grinned at me. "Good, huh?"

I nodded and beamed at the handyman. "You should be a baker, Fletcher. I think these are the best scones I've ever tasted."

Fletcher met my eyes shyly and a smile twitched his lips, then he quickly looked down again.

Barb the receptionist stuck her head into the room. "Fletcher, any chance you can fix the cabinet door in the toilet before you leave? It's falling off the hinges."

"I will fix it now," said the big man. He grabbed a couple of tools from his bag and lumbered out of the room.

"Another scone?" said Cassie, offering the paper bag to me. I was about to reach out when I noticed that Fletcher's tool bag on the floor was wriggling in the strangest way.

I pointed. "Uh... Cassie... is there something in that bag?"

She glanced down just as a little furry head popped out of the bag. I jumped back with a yelp, then realised—as Cassie fell about laughing—that it was only a cat. A little grey tabby cat with enormous green eyes, black eyeliner, and a little pink nose.

She looked up at me inquisitively. "*Meorrw*?"

"That's Muesli," said Cassie, still laughing. "She belongs to Fletcher and she goes everywhere with him. She's really friendly." She bent down and patted the little cat. "Want to say hello?"

"Er... No, thanks," I said, eyeing the feline askance.

"She won't bite, you know," said Cassie with a smile.

"It's not that," I said quickly. "I just... well, you know, I've always been more of a dog person. I'm not... I'm not really into cats." I tried to edge away surreptitiously.

Muesli, of course—like a typical cat—decided that she was most interested in the one person who wanted nothing to do with her. She hopped out of the tool bag and scampered towards me, her tail straight up in the air and her whiskers quivering. I hastily took a few more steps back.

"*Meorrw?*"

I looked determinedly at the ceiling, hoping that if I pretended I couldn't see her, the little cat would go away. Something touched my legs. I sneaked a peek downwards. Muesli was rubbing herself against my shins.

"She's not going to pee against my legs, is she?" I asked in alarm.

"Of course not—she's not a dog!" said Cassie in exasperation. "She just wants to say hello. Give her a pat, Gemma."

I hesitated, then reached down and tentatively touched the top of Muesli's head. The fur was softer than I expected. I stroked between her ears with one nervous finger.

"Tickle her under her chin—cats like that," said Cassie.

I hesitated again, then did as Cassie directed. A soft rumbling sound filled the air as Muesli nuzzled her chin against my fingers.

Cassie smiled. "Aww... see? She's purring." She put the bag of scones down and dusted off her hands. "Well, I'm off to teach my class now. Can you hang around here until Fletcher gets back, just to keep an eye on Muesli—"

"Wait—you're... you're leaving me alone with the cat?" I said.

Cassie gave a shout of laughter. "Anyone would think that I was leaving you alone with a sabre-tooth tiger! She's only a little cat, Gemma. You'll be fine."

With another laugh, she was gone and I was alone in the room with my new feline friend. I stared at the grey tabby warily. She stared right back at me, her green eyes wide and curious. *Okay, no need to worry. There's nothing to this cat-sitting gig*, I assured myself. *All I have to do is more of that chin-tickling thing...* But as I reached out again, Muesli suddenly turned and began trotting towards the door.

"Hey—wait—no, what are you doing? Muesli, come back!" I said, running after her.

She gave me a cheeky look over her shoulder and waited until I was almost on top of her. Then, just as I was swooping down to grab her, she darted to the right, out of my reach.

"*Ow!*" I winced as my knees landed with a painful thump on the hard wood floor of the studio. Irritably, I looked around. Muesli had disappeared through what looked like a gap in the studio wall. On closer inspection, however, I realised that it wasn't a gap but rather a concealed cupboard door which was slightly ajar. I pulled it open and found myself staring at a small storeroom which had been built into the wall. It was filled to bursting with cardboard boxes stacked high, stage props piled on top of one another, dance costumes crammed on racks, and freestanding ballet barres.

"Muesli?" I called hesitantly.

"*Meorrw!*" came the insolent reply, somewhere deep in the pile of props. She sounded like she was daring me to come and get her.

Little minx. I scowled. She'd done that last-minute escape trick thing on purpose, just to make me nearly fall on my face. I rubbed my sore knees. *Wait until I get my hands on you.* Then I surveyed the mess piled in front of me and frowned. How on earth was I going to find her? I reached in and carefully lifted out a pair of fairy wings, followed by a polystyrene toadstool mushroom and a couple of pairs of ballet shoes, their pink ribbons trailing dust. The boxes behind them wobbled precariously and a mini disco-ball rolled out of the top box and bounced on the floor.

I sneezed. There was the sound of scrambling from deeper within the pile. I peered into the back of the storeroom. Was that a furry grey tail?

"*Meorrw!*"

Aha! I pounced, reaching out to grab her. A cloud of dust billowed up, causing me to sneeze again and stumble sideways. My shoulder hit the stack of boxes and I flailed, spinning and falling backwards into them.

"Aaaaagghh!"

I crashed to the floor of the storeroom, the boxes

tumbling down around me, spilling their contents everywhere. Something hit me on the head with a soft thud, then bounced to the floor. I looked down. It was a plastic jar of glitter—and it had just emptied itself on my head. I coughed, then struggled to my feet and staggered out of the storeroom.

"Oh my goodness, whatever happened to you?"

Barb the receptionist stood staring open-mouthed at me. She had obviously heard the commotion and come to investigate. I turned and caught sight of myself in the mirrors on the opposite wall. I looked like Sparkly Swamp Thing. I was covered head to toe in pink glitter.

"A...harr...nacksiden..." I mumbled, trying to speak through a mouthful of shimmering grit. "Bloorry ca—!"

There was a small thud behind me and a little furry grey shape jumped down from a box at the back of the storeroom, and strolled nonchalantly out.

"*Meorrw*?" she said, looking up at me innocently.

Barb looked like she was trying not to laugh. Slowly, she helped me pile everything back into the storeroom, then she found some sticky tape and tried to get the glitter off my hair, skin, and clothes. When Cassie returned forty-five minutes later, she found me still sulkily trying to pick glitter off my cheeks while Muesli sat smugly next to me.

"Barb told me what happened," she said, trying to keep a straight face.

"Yes." I glared at her. "And you know glitter—it

never comes off!"

"Hey, at least you won't need to wear reflective gear when cycling at night," Cassie chortled.

I gave her a look, then said a frosty goodbye to Fletcher and Barb, and stomped out of the studio. Cassie followed me, still laughing.

"So... don't tell me you're not smitten with the kitten?"

"You're joking, right?" I said sourly. "Right now I'd like to wring her little neck!"

Cassie chuckled. "Give it time. I'm sure you'll fall in love with Muesli. Everyone does."

"Not me," I muttered.

Cassie gave me a smug smile. "We'll see. No one can resist that little cat's charms. You should have seen what it was like last Saturday morning when the ladies arrived for yoga class and Fletcher was there with Muesli. They went bananas over her. I told Fletcher he should have charged people to give her a cuddle—he could have made a fortune." She caught my arm. "Anyway, what do you think of him, Gemma?"

"Of Fletcher?" I looked at her in surprise. "Well... He seems really nice. I mean, I didn't really get to know him—he's so shy and quiet. He hardly talks."

"Yeah, that's typical Fletcher. Even when he gets to know you better, he won't say much. But isn't his baking divine?"

I nodded. "Oh my God, yes! I'm sure I've ruined my appetite for dinner with that scone but it was totally worth it!"

"That's why I thought he'd be perfect!" said Cassie triumphantly.

I looked at her in puzzlement. "Perfect for what?"

"As a baker!" said Cassie.

I frowned at her. "I don't understand. What—"

"For your tearoom, silly!" said Cassie. "You're not thinking of doing the baking yourself, are you?"

I gave her a rueful grin. Cassie knew me too well. Much as I enjoyed *eating* delicious baking, creating it myself was a whole different matter. I knew my limits and no, I wasn't risking the success of my new business by trying to do the baking myself.

"I was thinking you could hire Fletcher," said Cassie.

"Well, I was thinking of hiring someone from London..." I said doubtfully.

"At London salaries?" said Cassie, raising an eyebrow. "You'll go through your savings in a month, Gemma! Besides, I think everyone in the village has been worried that you might bring in some poncy French chef or something."

"Of course not, I'm going to be serving good old-fashioned British baking—just like our great-grandmothers used to bake."

"Well, that's exactly what Fletcher does. If you want mouth-watering, traditional British baking, then Fletcher's your man."

"I'll think about it," I said.

"Do," said Cassie, adding with a twinkle in her

eye: "And just think—you'll be getting little Muesli into the bargain."

CHAPTER TEN

I considered it a small achievement that I managed to drag myself out of bed by ten-thirty the next morning, although I still felt like a creature that had been dug out of hibernation. I came blearily down to the kitchen where I found my mother looking as immaculately groomed as always, her hair done up in an elegant coil and her fine wool dress protected by a large white apron.

"Good morning, darling!" she sang as I stomped in and perched grumpily on one of the kitchen stools. I wasn't a morning person at the best of times and the jetlag had made me extra grouchy.

"What would you like for breakfast, dear? Although it's really almost lunchtime..."

"I'm not hungry," I mumbled.

My mother tutted. "You know breakfast is the

most important meal of the day. How about some toast and marmalade? I have a fresh loaf here. Or perhaps you'd like some poached eggs? There's always cereal, of course, though I'm not sure I have the kind you like. I must pop to the supermarket and pick up some of your old favourites..."

As she was talking, my mother was busily laying things out on the counter in front of me. I stared at a large glass jar filled with strange, black, slug-like forms, which had been placed next to the marmalade.

"What on earth is that?" I asked, pointing to the jar.

"Oh, those are from Mabel Cooke, darling. Stewed prunes. Mabel says they are wonderful for the digestion. Remember she was telling you about them that afternoon when they came for tea? She dropped them off yesterday. Wasn't that nice of her? She said to tell you that she would be checking with you the next time she saw you, to see if the prunes had done their job."

Eeuuggh—the last thing I wanted to do was discuss the state of my bowels with Mabel Cooke and her cronies.

"Would you like me to put some in a bowl for you, darling?"

"No thanks," I said hastily. "I... I'll just have some cereal."

As I helped myself to milk and cornflakes, my mother said brightly, "Now, darling, you still haven't shown me how to get my email on the i-Tap. Helen Green has been reading all her emails and replying to them using hers—and did you know, you can even take photos with the i-Tap and *attach* them to an email and send them on!"

I sighed. "iPad, Mother. It's called an i*Pad*. Yes, all right, I'll show you."

Eagerly, she brought her iPad over and proudly turned it on. Then I watched in silent agony as she began trying to navigate her way around the screen.

"You have to tap on that little picture of the envelope, Mother," I said, trying to restrain my impatience as I watched her flick her thumb over the screen. "With the tip of your finger."

"I *am* tapping!" cried my mother, jabbing with her forefinger. "Nothing is happening!"

"Maybe you're not tapping it hard enough—you have to do it a bit firmer and in the centre of the mail icon... no... well, not like that... no, now you've tapped the icon next to it and opened up another app. Close that and go back to your homepage... no, that's not—okay, just ignore that... press the round button at the bottom of the iPad—that will take you back to the home screen... yes, that one... Now, try tapping on the little picture of the envelope again... yes, tap firmly in the centre..."

I swallowed a sigh as my mother stabbed ineffectually at the screen. I could see her getting more and more frustrated with each attempt, and struggling to follow her own dictate that a lady must never use "coarse language".

"Oh, shi...shipwreck!" she muttered, tapping the screen for the twentieth time. "No, not that... Oh, sh...sherbert!"

At this rate, she's going to run out of 'sh—' words, I thought wryly. Finally, after several more attempts and exclamations of "Oh shoebox!", "Oh shampoo!", "Oh shovel!" and "Oh Shakespeare!", my mother finally managed to open her Inbox, reply to a message (by mistake), forward another message (to the wrong person), and delete an email coupon from John Lewis Department Store that she had been eagerly waiting for. Still, it was considered a success and, flushed with the heady power of her great technological achievements, my mother demanded that I show her how to access the online edition of several newspapers.

"Helen says the *Cotswolds Post* has a great website and there's even a section on upcoming local events," she said eagerly. "Where do I find it?"

"Okay, I'll make a shortcut for you... and then you just have to click on the icon... there, that's the homepage with a menu across the top, see? Sports, finance, weather, leisure... and you have to tap on each word to take you to those sections. Or you can scroll down the homepage to see the latest articles—"

I broke off as a headline on the page caught my eye. I sucked my breath in sharply.

"Darling?" My mother looked at me quizzically but

I ignored her, snatching up the iPad so that I could read the article properly. The words swam in front of my horrified eyes:

"I DIDN'T MURDER HER OUT OF JEALOUSY!"
Main suspect in the Cotswold hotel murder tells all about sordid love affair with victim

"The bas—the beast!" I said, remembering my mother's presence. "I can't believe he wrote this! He's completely twisted my words!"

"What is it, darling?" said my mother. "Is it about that horrid murder at the hotel? Have the police made an arrest?"

"No, it's just a stupid story—nothing important," I said hastily. Quickly, I shut down the page and returned the iPad to her. "I've got to run, Mother—I've just thought of something I need to do. I'll see you later!"

I gave her a quick peck on the cheek and dashed from the room. Upstairs, I hurriedly showered and dressed, all the while fuming about the article. *I'll make him retract everything he said!* I thought furiously. *How dare he make those insinuations! These journalists are all total rotters! Who are these so-called "sources" he's quoting? I never spoke to anyone about anything at the hotel!*

My thoughts were interrupted by the shrill ringing of my phone. I picked it up, noting that it was a local number I didn't recognise.

"Is that Miss Gemma Rose?" said an officious voice at the other end of the line.

"Yes, that's me," I said.

"I'm calling regarding your application for the First Time Start-Up Business Loan."

I felt a surge of excitement. My tearoom! I'd almost forgotten about it!

"Oh yes! That's wonderful—thank you so much! I'll come straight into the branch this morning to sign the papers—"

"Miss Rose—excuse me, but you haven't heard what I have to say," the impersonal voice cut in. "I was calling to tell you that, unfortunately, we have decided to decline your loan."

"Wait... *what*?" I said, feeling like the breath had been knocked from my body. "What do you mean? The last time I spoke to someone in your department, he said it was practically all approved. His name was Mr Hicks. I want to speak to him—please put him on."

"Mr Hicks and I are colleagues," said the impersonal voice smoothly. "He is away at present. However, rest assured that I have taken over his responsibilities and have made a full assessment of your case. It is with regret that I have to inform you that the bank will not approve the loan."

I felt a sense of disbelief and horror wash over me. No, this couldn't be happening to me. Without the loan, there was no way I could afford to buy that tearoom and all my dreams, my future, were going up in smoke.

"But... but I don't understand," I stammered. "Why? Why should the application suddenly be rejected? It was all set to go through and Mr Hicks assured me that this was simply a formality. I'd provided all the necessary documents—"

"Your papers were all in order," said the impersonal voice. "However, in view of recent developments, the nature of your application has changed and, in particular, the risks involved."

"The risks? What risks? What recent developments are you talking about?"

"Your involvement in the murder case," said the voice primly.

"My... *what?*" My head spun. "But I'm not involved in the murder case! I just happened to sit on the plane next to the victim. That was just a coincidence and... and bad luck, you could say. There was no other connection between us!"

"That's not what we had understood... based on reports in the media."

"In the media...? You don't mean that ridiculous piece of tabloid nonsense in the *Cotswolds Post* this morning?" I demanded. "You can't believe that! That was just a bunch of made-up rubbish! I didn't say half of those things, and even the few things I did say were taken completely out of context. You can't reject my application just because of some malicious rumours!"

"As I said, we have made a full assessment of your

case and this is our decision. We are an old, reputable bank and we are very careful of the clients that we take on. I'm sure you understand the damage that could be done to the bank's reputation if it was discovered that we had provided a loan to a potential criminal—"

"But I'm not a criminal!" I roared. "This is absolutely ridiculous! I refuse to accept this!"

"There is an official appeals process," said the impersonal voice. "If you'd like to go through that, you can go to our website and click on the link—"

"Oh, stuff the appeals process!" I cried in frustration, slamming down the phone.

I sank down on my bed, despair washing over me. I couldn't believe how suddenly everything had gone wrong. It had seemed like my dream was coming true: coming back to Oxford, seeing the tearoom in Meadowford, even meeting a possible baker... and now it was all being snatched away from me at the last moment. I bit down hard on my bottom lip as tears threatened.

Then I drew a long, shuddering breath and sat up straighter. No, I had given up too much and come too far to just let myself be beaten like this. I wasn't going to just meekly accept things. And sitting in my bedroom feeling sorry for myself wasn't going to get me anywhere. I sprang up. I was going to fight this. I was going to make the bank change their minds and approve the loan. But how could I do that?

By convincing them that I had nothing to do with

Jenn's murder.

I thought about my original plan to hunt down the journalist and make him retract his statement. But that wasn't enough, I decided. I needed someone with more authority than that—I needed the "official line". Someone to confirm that I wasn't a suspect.

The police.

Yes, I needed to speak to Inspector Glenn. He must have followed up on Andrew Manning by now— maybe they even had the young man in custody already. If I could speak to him and maybe get him to vouch for me, then I was sure the bank would reconsider.

Feeling suddenly much better, I finished dressing, then left the house, hopped on my bike, and cycled towards Oxfordshire Police Station.

CHAPTER ELEVEN

I arrived at the police station flushed and panting but still fired up by the courage of indignation. I marched into the front reception and asked the constable on duty to see Inspector Glenn of the Oxfordshire CID.

"Do you have an appointment?"

"No, but I'm helping him with a murder enquiry," I said boldly.

The constable gave me a suspicious look. "Have you come from a rave party or something?"

"No, why?"

"You're sort of sparkling."

I sighed. "I had an accident with some glitter at a dance studio."

He gave me another suspicious look but put the call through. A few moments later, I was shown into an interview room where Inspector Glenn joined me.

"You saved me a trip, Miss Rose," he said without preamble. "I was just about to head out to North Oxford to see you. I have some more questions for you."

I decided to dispense with the niceties as well. "Have you seen the article in the *Cotswolds Post*?" I demanded. "It's outrageous what they're saying about me! How can they call me a murder suspect? It quoted 'police sources'... did you speak to that journalist?"

"I merely spoke the truth," said the old inspector, glowering at me. "As it happens, you *are* a suspect in this case. I'm sure I don't need to remind you that you were the last person to see the victim alive. We have witnesses who confirm that you left the hotel lobby with Ms Murray under suspicious circumstances—"

"What do you mean 'suspicious circumstances'?" I said.

"According to witness reports, the victim appeared confused and unsteady on her feet."

"She was drunk! That's why I was helping her to her room! My goodness, I was just trying to do a good turn—why do people have to give it a nasty interpretation?"

The inspector continued as if I hadn't spoken. "And then, of course, there is the question of your relationship with Ms Murray."

"There *was* no 'relationship'," I said angrily. "I

think you're just fishing for a motive because you want to pin the murder on me and anything will do."

"How can you explain your quick intimacy with the victim, if you only just met on the plane?"

I gave him a withering look. "Have you never heard of friendship? People meet each other, find that they have something in common, that they enjoy chatting with each other, and lo and behold—they become friends. What's so strange about that?" I shook my head in frustration. "You should be after the *real* murderer instead of wasting time questioning me. Andrew Manning—have you checked up on him? If you want suspicious behaviour, he's got it in bucketloads! If you ask me, he had far more reason to harm her. It's well known that some men can't stand being rebuffed by a woman. His pride couldn't take it. He came down fuming, filled himself up with Dutch courage, decided he was going to make Jenn pay for rejecting him, and went back up to her room. Maybe he didn't intend to kill her but they had an argument and he lost his temper and hit her on the head."

The inspector sat back and regarded me quietly for a moment. I had an impression that he was deciding what to say. Finally he said, "We *have* questioned Andrew Manning."

"And?" I said eagerly.

"He admits that when you saw him, he *had* just been to Jenn Murray's room."

"Aha!" I said, leaning forwards. "You see? He must

have—"

"He also said that he found her door slightly ajar and that when he pushed it open and went in, he found her already dead."

I froze. "Already dead? But that's... that's impossible! She was alive and well when I returned with her handbag. Andrew Manning is lying!"

The inspector said nothing.

I looked at him in frustration. "Don't you see he must be lying? He's just saying that to cover his own back! If he says that she was already dead, then it gives him an alibi for later, when he actually did kill her. In fact, that probably explains why he went back down to have the drink at the bar—so that everyone could see him and confirm that he had come back downstairs. I left Jenn at eleven and you said she was dead by eleven-thirty so Andrew Manning must have gone back up again and killed her. But by saying he found her body earlier, it means that he couldn't be accused of killing her later—because she was 'already dead'."

"Then why admit he went to her room at all?" asked the inspector.

"He probably wouldn't have, except that he knew that I had seen him—so he had to come up with something and this fit his carefully prepared alibi. See, originally, he wouldn't have known that I was going back to Jenn's room—maybe he saw me leave and just assumed that I'd left for the night. He must have got a shock when I came back. That's probably why he looked so pale and shaken when he saw me step out of the lift—he suddenly realised that I might be going back to Jenn's room and then would be able to refute his carefully planned alibi."

The inspector still said nothing. His silence was starting to make me nervous.

"Well?" I said. "Why won't you say anything? Don't you agree?"

He said coolly, "As it happens, Miss Rose, I'm inclined to believe Andrew Manning's story."

"What?" I said. "How can you possibly believe him? He was harassing Jenn earlier that evening, then I saw him practically coming from her room. And he has the room next to Jenn's. How can you believe his word that he didn't kill her?"

"I believe his word," said the inspector slowly, "because it's backed up by evidence from the forensic pathologist."

I looked at him blankly.

"The post-mortem results have come back and, according to the pathologist, the killing blow was struck by someone using the right hand."

"So?"

"So... Andrew Manning's right hand was in a sling. He couldn't have used it. And don't worry—we've confirmed that with the doctor. Therefore, he could only have used his left hand to deliver the blow—but that does not accord with the forensic evidence." He leaned forwards and said, his voice silky, "May I ask, are you left or right-handed, Miss

Rose?"

"Um... Right...right-handed," I stammered, hating the way I suddenly felt on the defensive. "What... Did they find out what the weapon was?"

"Yes, the heavy brass doorstop by the bedroom door. The murderer must have picked it up and used it to strike Ms Murray on the head."

"So were there fingerprints?" I asked eagerly.

"There were traces of skin and blood which matched Ms Murray's type. But no fingerprints. Of course..." The inspector gave me a cool look. "Nowadays, anyone with an ounce of intelligence would know to wipe their fingerprints off the murder weapon. Especially someone intelligent enough to have graduated from Oxford University."

I tried to ignore the pointed way he said that. Instead, I went back to my earlier point. "If Andrew Manning really found her dead, why didn't he call the police? Why did he just leave and say nothing about it?"

"He said he was scared. He realised that he had been seen harassing Jenn earlier in the evening and he panicked. So he just backed away and rushed downstairs and tried to forget the whole thing."

"Aww, come on—surely you don't believe that? He finds a dead body and says nothing about it, does nothing all night, other than have a couple of stiff drinks?"

Inspector Glenn shrugged. "It happens. People have strange reactions sometimes when they come across a murder—some people simply shut down and try to pretend they never saw anything. Mr Manning knew that the body would be discovered by Housekeeping in the morning so it wasn't as if it would lie there undiscovered forever. He just didn't want to be the one to find it."

I shook my head. "It... it still doesn't make sense... I know Jenn was alive when I went back with her handbag, which was *after* Andrew Manning had left her room. So he *can't* have seen her dead. Why would he lie? There must be a reason!"

"There *is* a reason..." said Inspector Glenn, his eyes boring into mine. "I think the reason is that *you* are lying, Miss Rose."

I gasped.

The inspector continued relentlessly. "You say that we only have Andrew Manning's word that Ms Murray was already dead. By the same token, we only have *your* word that she wasn't. You've been very quick to tell everyone that Jenn was still alive when you left her room. But if we accept that Andrew Manning's statement is true, then that changes everything. Now I ask myself why you're so keen for everyone to think that Jenn Murray was still alive when you left her at 11 p.m. and the only reason I can think of is to establish an alibi for yourself."

I drew back sharply in my chair. "That's ridiculous!"

"Is it?" said the inspector. "Not to my mind. You see, we have always thought it very suspicious from the beginning that you took so long to come down to the lobby to search for the handbag."

"But I told you! That lift took ages to come and then there was a couple in it and—"

"Yes, we've questioned that couple and they don't remember the lift stopping on the third floor or seeing you waiting for it."

"Well, I'm not surprised," I said wryly. "They were so wrapped up in each other, I doubt they would have noticed if the whole hotel had fallen down around them."

Inspector Glenn leaned back in his chair and regarded me coldly. "What it amounts to, Miss Rose, is that, in reality, the last time any witness can confirm that Ms Murray was seen alive was when *you* were escorting her back to her room. After that, we only have your word—and Andrew Manning's word— as to when she was still alive. You both give differing accounts. Now given that Mr Manning has been cleared by forensic evidence as being unlikely to be the murderer, I am inclined to believe his account... which means that *you* are the one who's lying." He paused, then added, "It is interesting to note that there were no signs of forced entry, which means that Jenn must have known and trusted her attacker in order to let them into the room. Or... her murderer was someone who had gone into the room with her— perhaps a 'friend' who was helping her back from the bar after she had one too many drinks...?"

I felt the colour draining from my face.

"Are you arresting me?" I whispered.

The inspector gave me a predatory smile. "Oh no... not yet, anyway," he said. "I like to have things all tied up before I go in for the kill. But don't worry—I won't be long. Don't think you'll get away with this, Miss Rose."

I stood up shakily, nearly knocking my chair over. "I... I'd like to leave now."

"Of course." The inspector stood up as well and escorted me from the room with false courtesy.

I stumbled out of the police station and walked aimlessly down the street, my mind spinning frantically. My phone rang and I answered it mechanically. I was surprised to recognise the voice of the present owner of the tearoom.

"Gemma—I know we're not really supposed to communicate with each other, that we should leave things to the solicitors, but I wanted to speak to you directly." He paused, then said apologetically, "I know we'd already agreed on a price and we are still keen to sell to you, but you see... the Chinese have come in with a very generous offer."

My heart sank. "Yes, I... I'd heard from my friend."

"As I said, we would still like to sell to you, Gemma," the owner assured me. "It would be our first choice, in spite of the greater sum that the Chinese are offering."

"Thank you," I said earnestly. "I know everyone in the village really appreciates your efforts to preserve the integrity of the institution."

"Yes, well, of course. But the thing is... you see, I thought you had said previously that we would be finalising things today? But when I checked with my solicitor just now, he made some enquiries and it seems that the bank hasn't approved your loan?"

"Uh... it's just a temporary delay," I said quickly. "There's... there's been a bit of a misunderstanding, but I'm sorting it out now. Don't you worry—the money will be sorted and we'll be exchanging contracts soon."

He gave an embarrassed cough. "Well, I don't like to pressure you, Gemma, but we really do need to have things settled. The Chinese are becoming very insistent and they have said that if we don't accept their offer by tomorrow, they will be retracting it. I'm sure you can understand my position. If you're having trouble and unable to come up with the money, we can't afford to lose their offer."

I could feel myself sweating. "I just need a little more time... please," I said desperately.

He sighed. "Well, I suppose I could put them off one more day. As I said, we would really prefer to sell to you, Gemma. But I can't wait any longer than that—if I haven't heard from you by the day after tomorrow, I'm going to have the accept the Chinese company's offer."

I swallowed past the tightness in my throat. "Yes, I completely understand. And thank you—thank you for your understanding. I... I promise that I'll work something out."

I hung up and continued slowly down the street. My hands were trembling and I could feel my chest tightening, I felt like I couldn't breathe, everything was receding around me, and there was a roaring in my ears. *I'm having a panic attack*, I thought dimly. I staggered over to a nearby bench and sat down, putting my head between my knees. Slowly, my head cleared and my breathing steadied. I was about to sit up again when I heard a concerned voice.

"Gemma! Whatever is the matter, dear?"

I sat up to find myself surrounded by four little old ladies looking at me with concern. It was the Old Biddies. I realised that what I had thought was a bench was actually a bus stop and there was a group of people nearby, obviously waiting for the next bus, all eyeing me curiously.

Mabel, Glenda, Florence, and Ethel fussed around me.

"What is the matter, Gemma?"

"Aren't you feeling well, dear?"

"Did you have an accident?"

"Perhaps you need a nice cup of tea?"

The last comment brought a reluctant smile to my lips. Trust the English to always think that a cup of tea would fix everything.

I drew a shuddering breath. "I... I'm all right," I said with a weak smile. "Nothing's the matter."

"Nonsense! There's no fooling these old eyes. We can see that something is terribly wrong," said Mabel briskly.

Without waiting for me to answer, she grabbed my elbow, hoisted me up, and bundled me down the street, followed by Glenda, Florence, and Ethel. Before I realised what was happening, I found myself sitting in a little café in Oxford's Covered Market, with a steaming cup of tea in front of me.

"Here—have some sugar," said Glenda, heaping several teaspoonfuls into the cup.

"And some biscuits," said Florence kindly, placing a plate of shortbread biscuits next to the cup, while Ethel gently patted my back.

I wanted to protest but instead found myself obediently gulping the sweet hot tea and nibbling a crunchy biscuit. There was something strangely soothing about these mundane activities and, when I'd finished, I found to my surprise that I was feeling better.

"There now," said Mabel, eyeing me speculatively. "Nice to see a bit of colour back in your cheeks, dear." She paused and peered closer, then licked a finger and reached out towards me. "Is that glitter on your eyebrow? Here, let me—"

"No! No, thank you. I'm fine," I yelped.

She gave me a disgruntled look, then said, "Anyone can see that you're *not* fine, dear. Come now—tell us all about it. What's wrong?"

I opened my mouth again to protest that there was nothing wrong but instead, to my surprise, found myself pouring out the entire story—from my initial meeting with Jenn on the plane all the way to the

harrowing interview with Inspector Glenn at the
police station and the devastating phone call from
the tearoom owner.

"I can't believe Inspector Glenn thinks I'm the
murderer!" I fumed as I finished. "It's just so
ludicrous! It's as if he wants to pin the murder on
anyone and I'm the convenient scapegoat!"

Mabel nodded. "That's just what it is, dear, so
don't take it to heart. I've known Inspector Glenn a
long time—he used to be the village bobby, you know,
back in Meadowford-on-Smythe, before he worked
his way up—and I know his wife from church. Robert
Glenn is leaving for retirement next month and he
doesn't want an unfinished case on his record so he
just wants to wrap this up as fast as possible. Not
that he was ever great shakes as a detective
anyway—too quick to jump at any easy solution,
rather than going the extra mile to investigate things
properly."

"They say that his head is full of nothing else now
but his allotment and the cruise they're going to take
around Europe after he retires," said Florence. "My
neighbour's nephew works at the police station and
he says Inspector Glenn has been boring everyone
silly with his retirement plans."

"I heard that a young inspector is coming to take
his place—someone from up north. A really good-
looking fellow, from what I've heard," said Glenda
with a giggle.

"Who cares what he looks like? Let's just hope he's

a decent detective," I muttered.

"Well, how good a detective the new chap is, isn't going to help you now," said Mabel pragmatically. "The new inspector doesn't start for another month or so—so in the meantime, you will have to deal with Inspector Glenn. The thing is, Gemma dear, you don't have to sit back and just accept things."

"What do you mean?" I said, looking at her. "What can I do?"

Mabel made a *harrumphing* sound. "Really! Young people nowadays! Such defeatists! I thought you were made of sterner stuff, Gemma." She leaned forwards and said impatiently, "You can solve the case yourself, of course!"

I stared at her. "Solve the case myself? You mean, look for the murderer?"

"Why not?" said Mabel. "You've got a good head on your shoulders—don't tell me that Oxford education was wasted on you. Why shouldn't you start your own investigation?"

"Because I'm not a detective," I said. "I wouldn't know the first thing about detecting or whatever it's called."

Mabel tutted. "It's very simple, dear. Just get nosy and ask questions!"

"But I'm not the police—I don't have the authority to go around prying into things."

Mabel made an impatient sound again. "Really, Gemma! It looks like we'll have to show you how it's done. Come on, off we go."

"Where?"

"To the Cotswolds Manor Hotel." Mabel glanced at the clock on the wall. "Ah... perfect. It's lunchtime now and I should imagine that the lobby area will be very busy. Come on—we have no time to lose!"

CHAPTER TWELVE

Some forty minutes later, I found myself following the Old Biddies into the Cotswolds Manor Hotel lobby. As Mabel had predicted, the place was humming with activity—new guests checking in, old guests leaving, bellboys pushing trolleys of luggage around, and visitors coming to the day spa, to play golf, to have "All Day English Afternoon Tea" in the lobby lounge, with its view of the picturesque Cotswolds hills in the distance. The clink of fine china and the happy hubbub of conversation filled the air, as people drank tea and admired the dainty little finger sandwiches, cakes, and scones served on the silver three-tiered cake stands.

The Old Biddies scurried across the lobby and huddled behind a large potted palm a few feet away from the reception desk, with me hurrying in their wake. Mabel peered around one large palm leaf, then pointed to the door behind the reception counter and hissed:

"That's where the police have set up a temporary Incident Room."

"How did you know that?" I said, impressed.

"Village gossip," said Mabel, as if that explained everything.

And maybe it did. Although my childhood memories of life in Meadowford were pretty hazy, I did remember my mother often complaining about how everyone seemed to know your business—you could barely sneeze before the news had been spread to the other side of the village!

"Come on..." said Mabel, starting towards the reception. "We must look through the police reports for clues."

"Wait—you're not going to snoop through police documents?" I said, aghast.

Mabel gave a dignified sniff. "Whoever said anything about 'snooping'? We are simply looking for Mr Sutton, the hotel manager, and happened to go into his office. It is certainly not our fault if there are papers on the desk and we happen to glance at them."

"But..." I started to say again, but my protests fell on deaf ears. The Old Biddies were already toddling purposefully towards the reception.

I scurried after them, half appalled and half

disbelieving. I just couldn't believe that they were really going to sneak into the inner office. There was a single girl on Reception, head bent over the computer, her nails clacking away on the keyboard. She was facing the other way and Mabel kept a beady eye on her as we sidled past the opposite end of the long reception counter and stepped behind it. Luckily, the door to the inner office was at this end, barely a few steps away.

Mabel gave a final furtive look around then, quick as a flash, darted into the doorway. I didn't think anyone in their eighties could move so fast. The other three followed her, leaving me standing by myself.

A minute later, Mabel popped her head back out. "Don't just stand there like a lemon!" she hissed. "Everyone will see you!" She grabbed my arm and yanked me inside after them.

I stumbled through the doorway and glanced around. It looked pretty much the same as yesterday when I had come in to sign my statement, except perhaps with more reports and witness statements stacked on the desk. The Old Biddies hurried over and began rifling through the papers, bumping into each other in their haste.

"You do that pile," said Mabel bossily. "I'll look through the reports here."

"No, *I* want to do that pile," said Ethel, jutting her bottom lip out. "I'm the ex-librarian. I can read faster than any of you."

"You also forget faster than any of us too," said

Glenda under her breath.

"Oh bother... I haven't got my glasses," said Florence, holding a witness statement at arm's length and squinting at the small words on the paper. "Can you read that, Glenda, dear?"

Glenda peered owlishly at the paper. "Can you hold it a bit further away?"

I didn't know whether to laugh or cry. *This is a crazy idea. Do they really think a bunch of geriatrics could solve a murder?* Besides, I had a sneaking suspicion that their enthusiasm had less to do with helping me and more to do with the chance to poke their nose where they shouldn't. From their flushed cheeks and the excited gleam in their eyes, it seemed that the Old Biddies were positively *delighted* at this opportunity to meddle in a murder investigation.

Then I felt a wave of shame. What was I doing standing here, belittling their efforts? At least they were doing something! And they weren't even under suspicion themselves. Their futures weren't at stake and yet here they were, giving it their all. How could I make fun of their efforts when I hadn't done anything so far except splutter in indignation and feel sorry for myself?

Feeling chastened, I turned to the pile of papers on the filing cabinet nearest to me and began rifling through them. I realised that they were various pieces of information about Jenn herself—a copy of her hotel booking, some bills, several pages of notes gleaned about her from interviews with the hotel staff and guests, a communication from the Australian police confirming that a work colleague had identified Jenn's photo... I spied an Australian passport tucked into a clear plastic wallet and pulled it out, flipping it open to the ID page. A picture of Jenn stared solemnly back at me. On an impulse, I pulled out my phone and quickly snapped a picture. Just as I was returning the passport to the plastic wallet, I suddenly heard the sound I had been dreading.

The sound of footsteps in the doorway.

I dropped the passport back on the pile and froze like a frightened rabbit, my eyes darting frantically around the room. *What should we do? Where could we hide?* I looked across at the sash window. *Could we climb out of the window in time?*

Then I heard an exclamation and turned guiltily around. Derek Sutton, the hotel manager, was standing in the doorway, staring at us in astonishment. But it was the person behind him who made my heart stop. It was Inspector Glenn and his face was like thunder.

"What are you doing in here?" he demanded, pushing Derek Sutton out of the way and coming into the room.

"We came to see Mr Sutton," said Mabel grandly. She sailed forwards, completely ignoring the detective inspector, and wagged a finger at the hotel manager. "We have been waiting for you a very long time, young man!"

Inspector Glenn looked nonplussed. He opened his mouth but didn't seem to know what to say. Mabel took advantage of his confusion to continue blithely to Derek Sutton:

"We wanted to ask you about hiring out the hotel ballroom for the Meadowford Ladies' Society lunch next month."

"The... the hotel ballroom?" said Derek Sutton. "Er... are you sure? It's normally reserved for large weddings and banquets. It's... er... very expensive to hire."

"Well, in that case, you had better give us a special discount, hadn't you?" said Mabel tartly. She turned as if to go but the young detective sergeant, who had followed Inspector Glenn into the room, stopped her.

"Wait a minute—" he said with a suspicious look at the desk behind us. "All the papers on the table have been disturbed. Have you been snooping through the reports?"

"What reports?" said Mabel with the most perfect display of innocent surprise. The woman deserved an Oscar. She picked up a piece of paper from the desk and looked at it. "Is this something important, Sergeant?"

He snatched it from her hand. "It's a witness statement," he said testily. "This is all confidential information pertaining to a murder enquiry."

"Are you suggesting that I would pry into official police matters?" Mabel glared at him. "And there is no need to take that tone with me, young man. Is that how you speak to your grandmother?"

The young sergeant flushed and seemed to shrink inside his clothes. "N-no," he stammered, dropping his eyes. "I... I'm sorry, ma'am. I didn't think... Of course, you wouldn't..."

"Humph!" said Mabel, glowering at him. "I shall write to the Police Commissioner and tell him that I find the standards of conduct in the modern police force absolutely appalling. Good day!"

Bristling with offended dignity, Mabel marched out of the room, followed by the other three Old Biddies. I tried to scurry after them but Inspector Glenn's voice stopped me in my tracks.

"Just a minute, Miss Rose..."

I turned reluctantly back to face him.

"What are *you* doing in here?" He growled. "Don't tell me you came here with Mrs Cooke and the others—I know you're not in the Meadowford Ladies' Society."

I looked wildly around. "I... uh... I came to see Mr Sutton as well!" I said, glancing over at the bewildered hotel manager. "I... um... wanted to ask him... I left something of mine in Jenn's room that night and I wanted to see if I could get it back."

"You didn't mention this yesterday when I took you to look over the room," said Inspector Glenn, his eyes hard.

"Yes, I... um... forgot. You know, the shock of Jenn's death..."

"Very well—you can tell us what it is now."

"Oh... actually, don't worry about it. I can see that you're all very busy right now. I'll get it some other time," I said quickly, making as if to leave the room.

"No, I insist," said Inspector Glenn. His voice was soft but I could hear the veiled threat in there. "What is the item?"

Blast, I thought as I felt all eyes in the room on me. How was I going to get myself out of this mess now? I had said the first excuse that had come to mind but now if I didn't come up with something that could genuinely be found in Jenn's room, I'd be stuffed. It was bad enough being found in the police Incident Room when I was already the top suspect in this case. I had to convince Inspector Glenn that I really had come to see the hotel manager. But what could I say?

I closed my eyes for a second, desperately trying to recall what I had seen in Jenn's room. Something in the bathroom, I thought—anything—there were so many things on that vanity counter, the police would never know if I said one of them was mine. I dredged up my memory of what I had seen in the bathroom that day: *a little group of creams and lotions, a quilted gold cosmetic bag, a wooden hairbrush and a couple of elastic hair ties, the electric toothbrush standing forlornly by itself next to the sink...*

"A... a cosmetic bag!" I blurted out. "I... er... left a gold cosmetic bag in the bathroom."

I looked pleadingly at Derek Sutton, begging him with my eyes to help me.

He blinked, then a look of understanding came over his face and he smiled, saying quickly, "Oh, yes, right. I'll have Marie go and look for it. She's in charge of the rooms on that floor." He stepped over to the desk and picked up the phone, dialling an internal number. "Marie? Can you pop along to Room 302 and have look in the bathroom for a quilted gold cosmetic bag... yes, on the vanity counter, I think..." He glanced at me for confirmation and I nodded. "That's right. Can you bring it straight down, please?"

A few moments later, there was a knock on the office door and Marie the maid came into the room. In her hands was a gold cosmetic bag.

"That's it!" I said quickly, reaching out to take it, but the inspector intercepted me.

"I'm afraid I can't let you remove any evidence while the murder enquiry is still ongoing," he said, whisking the cosmetic bag out of reach.

"Oh, but you said..." I trailed off, confused as to why he let Marie bring it down in the first place.

He gave me a cold smile which didn't quite reach his eyes. "I like to call people's bluff, Miss Rose, and see if they're speaking the truth. In this case, I have my doubts as to whether this..." he held up the bag. "...*was* the real reason you came into this office but for the time being, I shall take your word for it. You can have it back when the investigation is over and all items are released. Until then, it will remain in police custody."

I murmured something in reply and, trying not to show too much relief, escaped the office a few moments later. As I stepped out into the lobby, I was accosted by the Old Biddies.

"Well! I think that was a very successful sleuthing mission," said Mabel with great satisfaction.

I stared at her. "What do you mean? It was a disaster! Not only did we not find anything useful, the police caught us snooping red-handed. You even abandoned me in there with Inspector Glenn," I said accusingly. "I was forced to concoct a whole bunch of lies just to convince him that I had an innocent reason for being in there." I heaved a sigh. "I think I lost five years off my life in the last ten minutes."

Mabel waved a dismissive hand. "It's good to have to think on your feet once in a while."

While I spluttered in indignation, Ethel gave me a soothing pat on the shoulder and said, "And we might have inadvertently discovered a very important clue, dear."

Glenda nodded eagerly. "Something we read or saw in there might point to the identity of the killer!"

"Well, it's not much use since we don't have copies of anything," I said sourly. "I doubt I could remember everything I glanced over—can you? Especially at your age—" I broke off, embarrassed.

But the Old Biddies didn't seem to take offence. Mabel smiled complacently and shook her finger at me.

"Just you wait, dear... you never know what you

might notice. You won't remember it now but your mind has probably stored it away, ready for a rainy day. And now..." She turned and surveyed the lobby lounge, patting her woolly white hair. "Those cakes look lovely. Shall we have some tea?"

CHAPTER THIRTEEN

I was ridiculously delighted, when I found myself awake the next morning, to see that the clock on my bedside table read 8:10 a.m. Progress! I lay for a moment, staring up at the ceiling, the events of the last few days drifting through my mind. Like watching a movie in reverse, I went back over everything that had happened until I was back on that plane, meeting Jenn Murray for the first time. I remembered the way she had been so nervous about flying; I remembered the tentative initial introductions, gradually warming into easy conversation and friendship.

I felt a sudden pang of regret. I hadn't known Jenn Murray well enough to really grieve for her when I found out about her death. I had been shocked and horrified, yes, but it hadn't really been *personal*. It was a distant sort of sadness, like hearing about an old school friend who had got cancer or a favourite high school teacher who had passed away. Now, however, for the first time, I felt a genuine sorrow at her death.

I had liked Jenn Murray. Perhaps we might even have become good friends. And it seemed terribly wrong that her life should have been cut short like this. Suddenly, quite apart from wanting to prove my own innocence, I wanted to get justice for Jenn. I wanted to find her killer and see them punished.

I sprang out of bed and hurried through my shower, grumbling as I kept finding more bits of glitter clinging to me. Then I hunted around my room for my favourite pair of jeans. I frowned. Where were they? I was sure I had left them there on the chair by the window, along with a bunch of other clothes that I'd been intending to wear again in the next few days. But looking at the chair now, I realised that the pile looked distinctly smaller. In fact, I could see that several things seemed to be missing. I was sure I hadn't put them away (no point hanging stuff up or putting them back in drawers if you were just going to take them out again soon—that's my motto) so where had they disappeared to?

Then I realised. *Of course, my mother.*

Just like when I was still living at home, my mother had probably come in to my room and decided to take some clothes hostage in the laundry. Let's just say, my mother and I had very different ideas about when things needed a wash and especially when things needed to be ironed. Irritated, I hurried down the hallway to my parents' room. The door was open and I stepped in—reluctantly admiring the tidy elegance of the room, the bed beautifully made up with matching pillows and bedspread—and felt a twinge of guilt at my own slapdash efforts in the morning. My mother was in the en suite bathroom and I went over to the interconnecting door.

"Mother?" I shouted through the door, above the noise of water sloshing in the sink. I heard the electric toothbrush going and realised that she was probably brushing her teeth, following breakfast. I did a mental eye roll. My mother's idea of proper oral hygiene involved a full floss and brush after every meal—and I knew it was only a matter of time before she started trying to convert me to the same routine.

"Mother? Did you put my dark blue jeans in the wash?"

There came a garbled reply, which sounded like "Yes, darling."

I blew out a breath of annoyance and hurried downstairs. Maybe she hadn't loaded the machine yet and I could still rescue them from the laundry hamper. I rushed into the kitchen and stopped dead.

My mother was standing at the kitchen counter, peeling potatoes.

"Good morning, darling!" She smiled as she looked up. "I thought I might make a shepherd's pie for lunch—"

"Mother..." I went towards her, confused. "Weren't you just...? I thought you were upstairs in your bathroom?"

"Oh, no, that must have been your father. He's just gone back upstairs to get ready for his meeting this morning and—why, whatever is the matter, Gemma?"

I stared at her, my thoughts whirling. In my mind's eye, I could see myself standing outside Jenn's door: sticking my head in through the door, leaving the handbag on the side table, calling out to Jenn. She had replied to me from the bathroom... or at least, I'd *thought* she had. Just as I'd thought my mother had replied to me from her bathroom just now—when it fact, it wasn't her at all. And yet, garbled and muffled by the electric toothbrush, my father's reply had fooled me...

I thought back to my second interview with Inspector Glenn. He had been convinced I was lying because forensic evidence supported Andrew Manning speaking the truth. But *I'd* been convinced that I was speaking the truth—that Jenn had been alive when I returned to her room with her handbag. I had been certain of it because I had heard her speak to me from the bathroom...

But now I wondered...

Leaving my mother staring after me, I turned and walked slowly back upstairs to my bedroom, deep in thought. What if... what if I *had* been wrong? Or rather, what if I had been misled? In other words, what if I had been given the *impression* that Jenn was alive—by somebody in the bathroom, pretending to be her? It was difficult to distinguish voices when someone was speaking with a toothbrush in their mouth—especially an electric one with the mechanical buzz further muffling their words…

It was the murderer who had been in Jenn's bathroom and who had called out to me.

The realisation made me sit down sharply on my bed. So if what Andrew Manning had said was true, Jenn must have been murdered not long after I left her room the first time. Her room was at the end of a long L-shaped corridor, with the lift at the other end. And there was a staircase near her door. Someone could have easily come up via the stairs and slipped into her room, even while I was standing at the other end of the corridor, waiting for the lift to come. Because of the bend of the L-shape, I wouldn't have seen the murderer entering her room, even supposing that I was looking. And the stiff lock on Jenn's door meant that when I pulled the door to, the latch might not have caught, leaving the door slightly ajar. That would explain why there were no signs of forced entry.

So the murderer had slipped into the room and killed Jenn. But just as they were about to leave, Andrew Manning had showed up at the door—which was once again slightly ajar because the stiff lock hadn't latched again. The murderer ducked quickly into the bathroom and waited while Andrew Manning walked in and found the body... but luckily for them, Andrew hadn't raised the alarm. Instead, he just ran away.

Then the murderer must have moved Jenn's body to the bathroom. And just at that point, I returned with Jenn's handbag. Again, their luck had held because instead of coming all the way in, I had simply stuck my head through the door and called out to Jenn. The murderer must have been a quick thinker, I marvelled, to have the presence of mind to immediately switch on the electric toothbrush and use that as a way to disguise their voice and fool me into thinking that Jenn was still alive.

But who was it? I wondered in frustration. I knew now that it couldn't be Andrew Manning but who else could it have been? Someone from the hotel? I tried to think back on our conversation—aside from Andrew, who else had Jenn complained about or mentioned having a problem with?

I sighed. My mind was blank. But I'd decided that I couldn't just sit around waiting for the police to solve the case. There was the looming deadline with the Chinese offer for the tearoom. I had to find the real killer, if only to prove my innocence to the bank and get them to approve the loan. Besides, while yesterday's escapade with the Old Biddies had been stressful, yes, in a way, it had been empowering too. Just to be doing something, to take Fate into your own hands, instead of sitting around being a victim.

But what should I do? Where should I start? Then it struck me. The answer lay with the murder victim: Jenn Murray herself. There had to be a reason she had been killed. This wasn't a random mugging in the street or a robbery gone wrong—this had been a calculated, cold-blooded murder. Somebody had wanted Jenn Murray out of the way.

But why? Who was Jenn Murray and why was she important? I thought back again to our meeting on the plane. If I was honest with myself, I had felt all along that there was something mysterious about Jenn, the little things that didn't quite add up. Like the way she had spoken about Oxford, mentioning the colleges with almost casual familiarity and yet claiming that she had only visited as a child and was a relative stranger... I sat up straighter as I remembered something: that story she had mentioned about the college cat at Locksley College— each kitten being given the same name and always being chosen to be the same colour... that was the kind of "insider trivia" that was only really known by a member of the University. A member of the college, in fact.

Had Jenn been a member of Locksley College? A student, perhaps, or a member of the faculty? I had no proof but I was willing to bet that was the case. How could I find out? I chewed my lip, thinking. I certainly wasn't going to go through all the college records for the last twenty-odd years, searching for her name. And in any case, it might not have even been her real name. If she had deliberately concealed her past connection with Oxford, she might have lied about her name too. Or perhaps not lied, I conceded—remembering her passport and the positive ID from the Australian police—but maybe she had changed her name.

I snatched up my phone from the bedside table and quickly brought up the picture I had surreptitiously taken yesterday of Jenn's passport. I looked down at her photo, noting the sun-bleached blonde hair, the tanned skin with premature wrinkles and age spots. She looked older than her forty-odd years, something that was fairly common in Australia's relentless sun, particularly if she had been a keen sun-worshipper. I wondered how much she had changed from her younger self. Would she have looked very different as a younger woman? Thinner? Paler? Darker hair? If I took this picture into Locksley College, would anyone still recognise her?

I could try, I thought doubtfully. I knew that at Oxford, many of the college staff, such as the porters, often served for years, sometimes decades. It was a long shot but there was a chance that I might be able to find someone who had known Jenn. I looked down at the photo again and sighed. There was a better chance of anyone recognising her if she looked the way she used to when she was at Oxford— particularly if she had put on a fair amount of weight and changed her hair since. If only I could have a picture of Jenn as her "young self"...

Maybe I can! I thought with sudden excitement. I brought up my Contacts list on the phone and scrolled through quickly. *Bingo.* Steve Cairns— graphic designer and Photoshop artist extraordinaire. I had worked with him on several marketing campaigns in my old job and I had seen him do things with airbrushing which should be illegal. If there was one person who could "reverse time" in a photograph, it was Steve. I glanced at the clock and calculated the time difference to Sydney. Steve usually worked late. I might just catch him before he left for the day. Hurriedly, I put the call through and a few moments later was listening to a familiar Aussie drawl.

"Gemma! Good to hear from you—how's life back in England?"

"A lot colder," I said with a chuckle. "I'm missing the Sydney sunshine already. How're you doing, Steve? Are you still at work?"

"Yeah, you caught me just in time. Finishing up my last job for the day, then I'm outta here. Mate of mine's having a barbie and I'm supposed to be bringing the beer. Anyway, you didn't call me from the other side of the world just to ask me how I'm spending my arvo?"

I laughed. "Actually I called to ask you a favour. Listen, Steve, if I send you a picture, do you think you could do your Photoshop magic and make the person look a lot younger? Like recreate what they would have looked like twenty years ago? And if they were living somewhere that didn't have a lot of sunshine?"

"Sure, I could give it a go. What's this for? Not trying to pass yourself off as a spring chicken, are you? Twenty years back and you'd be barely a nipper, Gemma."

I laughed again. "No, it's not me. It's someone else... and it's rather urgent. Is there any chance you could do it before you leave work today? I know you've got your friend's barbecue but—"

"No worries, Gemma. Won't take me a minute. But this all sounds very mysterious. Urgent, huh? What's it for?"

I hesitated, wondering how much of Jenn's murder had been covered by the Australian media. Steve might make the connection when he saw the photo—but until he did, I was going to keep things low key.

"It's... um... a bit confidential. But I'll tell you the whole story later, Steve," I promised. "Please can you just trust me and do this without asking any questions?"

"Oooh... now you've got me really curious! Okay, send it over and I'll work on it now." His voice turned serious as he went into professional work mode. "It'll just be a rough approximation, though, Gemma—I won't have time to do any fine detail stuff. And it's just a guess, of course, based on the usual parameters of ageing, such as weight gain, pigmentation, and skin sagging."

"Yes, that's fine," I said. "I know it might not look exactly like her as a young woman but I just need a rough idea."

"Okay. And don't forget that you promised to tell me what this is all about!"

"Promise!"

I hung up and carefully cropped Jenn's passport photo out of the picture I had taken yesterday, then emailed it to Steve. Then I waited in an agony of impatience. Finally, I forced myself to tidy my room and return the rest of the pile of clothes to their rightful places in my wardrobe and drawers. It wasn't as if Steve would work any faster with me sitting on the edge of my bed, chewing my nails, and at least this made me feel a bit virtuous. I was delighted as I folded the last sweater to hear the email notification on my phone and I pounced on it, eagerly opening the attachments.

"Good on you, Steve," I murmured, smiling to myself.

He had done a fantastic job and had even given me three versions of a "young" Jenn: the first with her skin smoother and tighter, the eyes lifted and the cheeks fuller, so that she looked like she was in her twenties. Her hair was darker blonde, without the sun-bleached streaks, and her complexion was paler. The second version was similar but with Jenn as a brunette. And the third was blonde once again but this time with a lot less weight, so that her cheeks were hollowed out slightly and her nose seemed narrower.

I sent Steve a fervent thank you, then smiled again as I looked down at the pictures. Armed with these, I was sure I was going to solve the mystery of who Jenn Murray was.

CHAPTER FOURTEEN

When I arrived at Locksley College later that morning, however, and introduced myself in the Porter's Lodge, my confidence took a knock when both college porters shook their heads at the pictures on my phone.

"Sorry, luv. Never seen 'er before."

"Are you sure?" I persisted. "What about this one? Or this one as a brunette?"

Again, they shook their heads. My heart sank.

"She might not have looked *exactly* like this," I said desperately. "But doesn't anything about her look familiar to you? Please try to remember! It's really important. Is there any chance you might have seen her passing through, either as a student or a member of the staff?"

The first porter leaned forwards and peered at the

picture again, then shrugged. "If she 'ad, I don't remember 'er."

"If it were a long time ago, then it might've been before our time," said the second porter. He pointed to the first porter and himself. "We've only been here the last ten years or so. You need to be speaking to one of the old chaps."

"You mean, the previous porters? Where are they now?" I asked eagerly

"Old Charlie's dead," said the second porter, scratching his chin thoughtfully. "And Gerald's gone off to live in Spain."

"There's old Tom Dooley," the first porter spoke up. "'E was 'ere when I started. Used to know every single one o' the students by name. Amazing memory, that man 'ad. If anyone can 'elp you, 'e can."

"And where can I find Mr Dooley?" I asked, holding my breath and hoping they wouldn't say that he was living in a nursing home and completely senile.

"'E's down in Abingdon, lives with 'is married daughter. 'E'd be getting on now—got a dodgy 'ip, you know—but I think 'e's going strong otherwise. 'Ere..." The first porter pulled out his own ancient mobile phone and began scrolling through it. "I reckon I might have 'is number in 'ere somewhere..."

Thankfully he did, and a few moments later, I was putting a call through to Tom Dooley's daughter. She sounded a bit bewildered at my request but agreed readily enough to let me visit her father. She gave me the address and added:

"He's usually pottering around the garden in the mornings, unless it's raining. It would be a good time to catch him now."

I hopped back on my bike and cycled out to Abingdon-on-Thames, a little market town to the south of Oxford. I had no trouble finding the house and a kindly-looking old man with wispy white hair and drooping cheeks opened the door and surveyed me with rheumy eyes.

"Mr Dooley?" I said.

"Aye?"

"I was wondering if I could ask you a few questions... about someone you might have known at Locksley College?"

His eyes brightened at the mention of the college and he held the door open wider. "Aye, come in. You from Locksley?" he asked.

"No," I said as I stepped into the front hall. "Although I am—I was—a student at the University. At another college. But I'm... er... interested in someone who might have once been at Locksley College." I paused as I saw him staring at me strangely. "Is something the matter?"

"Eh? No, no... it is just that you seem to be very shiny."

Shiny? "Oh..." I gave a sigh. "I—er—had a bit of an accident with some glitter." I was beginning to sound like a broken record.

He gave me another odd look, but seemed to accept my explanation at face value and led me into a neat little living room and gestured me to sit down. "Fancy a cuppa?"

I perched on the couch next to him and gave him a smile. "No, thank you. I don't want to put you to any trouble. I just wanted to ask you, Mr Dooley..." I took my phone out and brought up the picture of Jenn, holding it out to show him. "Do you recognise this woman? Do you remember seeing her around the college during your time there?"

He peered at the photo for a long time, then shook his head. "No, don't reckon I've seen her before."

I was unprepared for the deep disappointment that stabbed me. Somehow, I had been so sure that this was the end of the road, that Tom Dooley would instantly recognise Jenn and tell me who she really was. I swallowed a sigh and began to take my phone back, then I thought of something. I scrolled through to the other two versions that Steve had done.

"What about this one? Or this one?"

He started to shake his head again, then paused, his eyes on the last picture, which showed Jenn much thinner. "That one looks familiar. Aye... I remember now. But she had glasses then. And her hair was shorter."

My heart beat faster. "So you're saying you do recognise this woman? That she used to be at Locksley College?"

The old ex-porter nodded. "One of them Fellows at the college. Interested in primitive people and how societies change... what they call anthropology, I think. Always going on about tribes and such."

I felt a surge of excitement. "So she was a Fellow in Social Anthropology and a tutor at the college? What else do you remember about Jenn Murray?"

He frowned. "Name wasn't Jenn Murray," he said. "She was called Lynn. Lynn Williams. That's right— Dr Lynn Williams. 'Twas very sad. Only been with the college a short time when the tragedy happened."

I stared at him. "What tragedy?"

He blinked, his old face showing mild surprise. "Her plane crashing, of course. It was her first big research trip—sabbatical, they call it, I think. She was going out to study one of them tribes in some faraway place... New Guinea. That's right, Papua New Guinea. Deep in the jungle. Had to take a small plane to get there. It crashed and they never found any of the survivors. Very sad, it was. The Principal of the college said Lynn had a bright future ahead of her. A real loss to the University."

I took a sharp intake of breath as an idea struck me.

"Are you all right, miss?" Tom Dooley looked at me in concern.

I blinked and pulled my mind back to the present. "Uh... yes, sorry—so, do you remember anything else about Jenn—I mean, Lynn Williams? Like, did she have any family in Oxford?"

The old ex-porter furrowed his brow. "She was only with the college a short time before she disappeared. Didn't really get to know her that well.

It was over twenty years ago. Wouldn't have remembered her, actually, except that she used to come to the Lodge and we'd have a yarn about those tribes of hers." He chuckled in remembrance. "She used to say that we were all barbarians deep down, beneath the fancy suits and posh manners."

"So you don't know anything about her family?" I said, disappointed.

"She wasn't from Oxford. Family was somewhere in Exeter, I think. She was married," he offered. "But she didn't talk about her husband much. Think he gave her some grief—bit of a wandering eye, if you know what I mean. Oh, and there was a younger sister. Came up to the college to see her once. Actually, I was really surprised to hear that they were sisters when Lynn introduced me—her being so fair and her sister being so dark, you know. Looked almost Italian or Spanish or something." He grinned suddenly at me. "Wondered if maybe her parents had brought home the wrong baby! But you always know your own, don't you? Even when they look totally different, like—you know your own family."

We talked a bit longer but Tom Dooley didn't have much else useful to tell me. Finally, I thanked him and left. As I was about to re-mount my bicycle, my phone rang. It was Cassie.

"Hey, Gemma—I was just calling to see how you were," she said. "You sounded so down last night. Have you heard from the inspector again? Or the bank?"

"No, but listen, Cassie, I think things are finally beginning to make sense!" Quickly, I told her about my revelation that morning with the electric toothbrush and then about my talk with Tom Dooley.

"So... are you saying that the woman who was murdered was really an academic at Oxford? But then how did she end up in Australia under a different name?"

"That's just it!" I said excitedly. "She went out on this research trip to Papua New Guinea, right? It's famous as one of the last places in the world where a lot of the population still live in tribes and primitive societies—it's like a haven for anthropological research. And guess what? It's about a hundred and fifty kilometres from the north tip of Australia. Really close. In fact, I remember a Sydney friend—who was a keen sailor—telling me that you could cross the water between them easily by a small boat on a calm day."

"Okay, but so what?" Cassie sounded puzzled.

"Well, supposing Jenn—Lynn Williams—had gone out on this research trip and her plane crashed in the jungle. There were no official survivors—everyone was presumed dead—but suppose Jenn hadn't died. Instead, she was rescued by one of the remote tribes and was looked after by them for weeks, maybe even months. And suppose she had a head injury and lost her memory—"

"You're doing a lot of supposing," said Cassie.

"Just bear with me," I pleaded. "So then finally,

months later, she emerges from the jungle and makes her way to Australia. By then, all the news about the missing plane with the Oxford academic would probably have been forgotten. And with her amnesia, Jenn would have no record of her previous life, no way to find her way back—"

"Hang on... wouldn't people have asked questions or noticed? I mean, even if the plane crash wasn't in the newspapers anymore, the story would still be around and—"

"Remember, this was over twenty years ago! We didn't have Google Search or social media everywhere. We didn't have smartphones. You couldn't just look up information on the internet; people couldn't share news across the globe as easily as they do now. And Jenn might have changed a lot after her stay in the jungle. If she arrived at a small port on the northern tip of Australia—some backwater town which didn't have the tight border control and immigration bureaucracy that we have these days—then she could easily have slipped through and joined the local community." I thought for a moment, then added, "In fact, her surname— Murray—that's a really common street name in Australia. Almost every city has a Murray Street. Maybe it was given to her by the local people when she couldn't remember her own name... and she became Jenn Murray."

"I don't know... It's all a bit far-fetched. It sounds like something out of a novel or a movie," Cassie complained.

"Yeah, well, you know what they say—truth *is* stranger than fiction sometimes. You've seen enough bizarre stories in newspapers to know that. And besides, the point is, this story fits the facts as we know it. I'm willing to bet that if the Australian police dug into Jenn's background, they'd find something just like what I said."

"So are you saying that Jenn lied all along about her name and her background?"

I thought back again to Jenn's vague comments about Oxford—she had mentioned "glimpses" in her memory. I had assumed that she was talking about her childhood but now I realised that she was probably speaking the literal truth. She really did just have "glimpses" of Oxford in her memory.

"No, I think Jenn was telling the truth—as much as she could remember of it," I replied. "Maybe something had happened recently back in Australia which had re-awakened her brain and triggered some memories. That was why she finally decided to make this trip back to England. And it would explain the strange combination of her being a stranger and yet knowing details about the Oxford colleges that only an insider could have known.

"And—" I added eagerly, "—this also explains her morbid fear of flying! That makes total sense now that I know she'd been through a plane crash. It's probably what prevented her from making the trip before now. But then suddenly, after twenty years in

Australia, her past was finally starting to come back to her—"

"So she started trying to discover her true identity," Cassie finished for me.

"Yeah... and somebody didn't want that," I said grimly. "Somebody wanted 'Lynn Williams' to remain buried in the past."

"You mean, somebody recognised her?"

"Yeah, even though Jenn didn't recognise them in turn. But they must have decided that they couldn't take any chance that Jenn might remember 'more' of her past." I took a deep breath. "So they killed her."

CHAPTER FIFTEEN

As I cycled slowly back to Oxford, I mulled over the conversation that Cassie and I had just had. Then my mind strayed back to what Tom Dooley had told me. I knew I should have gone straight to the police with this new information but a part of me balked at doing Inspector Glenn any favours. It was childish, I know, but after the way the inspector had treated me so far, I didn't even feel like speaking to him again. Besides, he was the police—he had every resource at his disposal. *Let him do his own investigating!* I thought resentfully. He should have ferreted out Jenn's background and connection to Locksley College by himself.

Still, what should I do now? I had solved the mystery of Jenn's true identity, yes, but that brought me no closer to finding her killer.

I sat back slightly, letting the bicycle freewheel as

I followed the curve of the road, whilst my mind went feverishly over the case again.

The murderer had to have been someone at the hotel, I decided. Jenn had gone there straight from the airport—therefore, the "someone" from her past who had recognised her must have been at the hotel. A guest? Or a member of the staff? I racked my brains again, trying to remember my conversations with Jenn. Who else had she mentioned from the hotel?

The maid Marie, I realised suddenly. That first time she had called me from the hotel, Jenn had complained about one of the maids. She said she had caught the woman rifling through her handbag—and didn't like the way the maid had been so inquisitive about her background. "Insolent", Jenn had called her. She hadn't mentioned a name but she had described the girl as "dark". Marie was dark—black hair, olive-skin, and those eyes—I remembered those sullen eyes. I was willing to bet that the maid Jenn had been complaining about was Marie.

That first day, when I had been with Inspector Glenn in the hotel room, I had opened the door to find Marie eavesdropping outside. I had also seen her later, downstairs in the lobby, with Brett Lyle the journalist, right before he had come to hound me with questions. Was she the one who had fed him—and the police—that ludicrous story about me and Jenn being lovers? If Marie was the killer, then that made sense—it would have been in her interest to push the suspicion onto me, especially as she would have known that I was the last person to go to Jenn's room the night she was killed.

And she could have easily done it, I realised, remembering that night again and the way Derek Sutton had complained about Marie leaving the reception desk unattended. The maid had burst out of the side door connecting to the staircase that led up to all the floors. The same staircase that came out right next to Jenn's room. Marie could easily have run to the third floor using the staircase, killed Jenn, hidden in the bathroom, and waited until I had left the room, then slipped out and used the staircase to get back down to the lobby again. With the lift being at the other end of the corridor, I would never have seen her. The timing fit perfectly.

But why would she have killed Jenn? What was the motive? What connection could there have been between Jenn Murray and a maid working in a Cotswolds hotel?

Then something Tom Dooley said came back to me: "...there was a younger sister. Came up to the college to see her once. Actually, I was really surprised to hear that they were sisters when Lynn introduced me—her being so fair and her sister being so dark, you know. Looked almost Italian or Spanish or something..."

Could Marie have been Jenn's sister? I frowned. Surely she was a bit young? But then, I didn't know the age difference between them. Tom Dooley had simply said "younger sister". There could sometimes be a decade or more between siblings.

But in any case, wouldn't Marie have been overjoyed to see her long-lost sister again? Why would she want to murder her?

I had to speak to Marie, I decided grimly. I leaned forwards over the bike and began pedalling harder, heading northwest out of Oxford and into the Cotswolds. I would go back to the Cotswolds Manor Hotel and find the maid now. That was the only way to get answers.

Besides, I had a vague feeling that there was something I had overlooked yesterday—something I'd read or something I'd seen while in that Incident Room. Maybe the Old Biddies were right and you did unconsciously pick up clues that you stored away without realising. Perhaps if I went back there, it would jog my mind and I would remember...

***

There was an eerie sense of déjà vu as I stepped into the hotel lobby: the same bellboys hurrying past with trolleys of luggage, the same smattering of guests by the reception desk, waiting to check in and check out, the same crowd of tourists congregating in the lounge, enjoying scones, cakes, and dainty sandwiches with pots of English tea. And even—I did a double take—the same four little old ladies huddled furtively by the potted palm tree. The Old Biddies.

What were they doing here?

I marched over to them and peered over their shoulders. "Hello."

They jumped guiltily, then looked at me in relief. "Oh, it's only you, dear."

"What are you doing here?"

"Sleuthing," said Mabel Cooke succinctly. "We were interrupted yesterday so we are back to finish the job."

"You're not going to try to get into the Incident Room again?" I said in disbelief. "The inspector will never believe any story you make up this time."

"Inspector Glenn's down at the station," said Mabel smugly. "I've checked that. He won't be coming to the hotel until after lunch. And his sergeant's with him. They've only left one constable on duty to guard the room and we've taken care of him." She smiled in a way that made me wonder what the poor officer had been sent off to do.

"What about Derek Sutton?" I said. "It was originally his office—he might be around."

"Oh, him." Mabel waved a dismissive hand. "We've sent that gormless hotel manager off to the ballroom to take some measurements... for our Meadowford Ladies' Society lunch," she explained with a twinkle in her eye. "We certainly can't hire the room until we know that it is of the right dimensions to accommodate our home-made cakes display."

Poor Derek Sutton, I thought with a sigh. "Okay, but I still think it's too risky. And besides, I thought you looked through the papers yesterday? What else do you think—"

"We didn't have time to go through them all," Florence protested.

Glenda nodded eagerly. "There were several interviews with the hotel staff and they were *so* interesting! Did you know that one of the golf-caddies has been having affairs with several of the lady guests? There was a picture of him and I must say, he's a *very* handsome young man. Oh, if only I were forty years younger..." she sighed.

"And Mrs Carson, the Maître D' in the restaurant, is actually *Miss* Carson," said Florence. "She just pretends to be married because she doesn't want anyone to know that she's still a spinster at fifty-five! And I always thought that Mr Sutton was divorced but it turns out that he's a widower, terrible tragedy, and Mr Sullivan of the concierge too. Although he's remarrying again later this year. And Miss Kerry, from the spa, is actually adopted and so she's not Irish at all!"

"And one of the bellboys is going on *Britain's Got Talent*," added Ethel. "He can whistle underwater, apparently. He has been practising the entire 'Flight of the Bumblebee' in the bathtub for his audition piece."

"What I want to know is if Mrs Carson really trained in Paris," said Mabel with a sniff. "Always putting on airs and graces and acting like she's better than everyone else..."

I made a noise of exasperation. "But what's all this got to do with the murder? You just want to snoop through people's backgrounds," I said. "None of these people have anything to do with Jenn! At the very least, you should have been looking at the interviews of the staff who had contact with her—" I broke off and gripped Mabel's arm urgently. "Mrs Cooke—did you read anything about a maid called Marie? What's her surname? Where's she from? Does she have any family?"

"Marie?" Mabel screwed up her face in an effort to remember. "No, I don't think so, dear..."

"We've got to get back in the Incident Room!" I cried, completely forgetting my own protests earlier. "I've got to find the notes on Marie and find out about her background. She's in charge of the floor with Jenn's room—surely the police must have questioned her in more depth. In fact, when she came down yesterday with that cosmetic bag—"

I broke off, sucking my breath in sharply.

Suddenly I realised what it was that had been nagging me—the "clue" that I had unconsciously picked up.

The answer that had been staring me in the face all along.

"Oh my God... I think I know who the murderer is..." I whispered.

CHAPTER SIXTEEN

The Old Biddies stared at me. "Gemma? Are you all right?"

Without answering, I turned and ran from the lobby. Following the signs, I ducked down the long corridor connecting the main building of the hotel to a large structure out in the grounds, which had originally served as the coach house, but which had recently been converted into a spacious ballroom. My shoes skidded on the polished wood floor as I came to a halt inside the ornately panelled room with its gilt-edged mirrors and graceful chandeliers.

Derek Sutton looked up from the far corner where he was crouched, a measuring tape in his hands.

I advanced towards him, breathing hard. "It was you, wasn't it?"

He rose to his feet. "I beg your pardon?" he said

pleasantly.

"You... you murdered Jenn Murray," I said, staring at him. "Or should I say, Lynn Williams, your wife?"

He froze. "I'm afraid I don't know what you're talking about," he said, still in that polite hotel manager voice.

"Oh, I think you do," I said. "You recognised her, didn't you? That night when she came down... you had been off a few days with the flu and had just come back on duty so you hadn't seen her check in, but when she came down to meet me, you recognised her instantly. I remember you seemed to act a bit weird, standing there staring at her, but I thought it was just because of her funny request for a hot water bottle. You must have had a bad moment until you realised that she didn't recognise you at all. Although..." I snapped my fingers. "I remember now! Jenn did mention that you looked familiar, when we were having drinks. She couldn't place you at the time, but her memory might have slowly come back. That's what you couldn't risk, wasn't it? That's why you killed her?"

There was a long pause, then at last Derek Sutton said, "Yes. I couldn't afford for her to suddenly recognise me and remember who she was."

"But why? Why would you want to kill your own wife?" I demanded. "You should have been overjoyed that she had returned at last. She had been lost in a plane crash, hadn't she? That was the 'terrible tragedy' that was mentioned in your police interview notes—and which had left you a widower."

"Yes, and that was years ago," said Derek Sutton savagely. "I'd paid my dues. Not that there had ever been much love lost between me and Lynn. Our marriage was a huge mistake. She told me before she left for her research trip that she was planning to divorce me when she got back. Then I got the news that her plane had disappeared in the jungle..."

"But I don't understand... Why would you want to kill her after all this time? However bad your marriage was, surely you couldn't hate your wife enough to want to harm her after all these years?"

"Oh, I didn't hate Lynn. Not anymore anyway," said Derek Sutton softly. "But I needed her dead."

"Why?" I looked at him in bewilderment.

"Because of the life insurance claim!" Derek hissed. "Lynn and I both took out life insurance when we first married—it was one of those silly, idealistic things you do when you're young and besotted and wanted to prove your love to each other. If she died, then I would get half a million pounds, and vice versa. After her plane went down and they thought there weren't any survivors, I put in a claim but the bastards refused to pay—they kept insisting that because a body hadn't been found, she might still be alive. Even after seven years—which is usually how long it takes to declare a missing person legally dead—they still wouldn't accept it. They just didn't want to pay out the half a million pounds and were trying to find any way to wriggle out of it."

"It's been a lot more than seven years," I pointed out.

"It's been nearly twenty," Derek said bitterly. "And even the insurance company had to admit that the chances of Lynn still being alive were pretty small after all this time. So they seemed to cave in at last. Last month, I got a letter out of the blue saying that they had finally decided to settle the claim. Providing everything goes as planned, I should be getting half a million pounds deposited into my bank account in two weeks' time." He leaned forwards and narrowed his eyes at me. "But that *wasn't* going to happen if Lynn suddenly turned up alive."

"So you murdered her?" I said, aghast. "Just because her return was... 'inconvenient'? How could you do that?"

He shrugged. "To all intents and purposes, Lynn was dead anyway. Everyone had accepted that and moved on. It wasn't as if I was suddenly depriving people of her presence."

"But you were still taking a life!" I said, shocked at his cold attitude. "You killed a woman in cold blood..."

"She never saw it coming. She was so woozy from the alcohol—so you needn't worry. She didn't suffer," he said callously. "In fact, I had the whole thing perfectly planned, and if you hadn't poked your nose in things, Miss Rose, no one would have been any wiser. How did you guess?" he asked suddenly.

"It was the cosmetic bag," I said. "When you rang Marie yesterday on the internal phone to ask her to bring it down, you described it to her as a 'quilted gold cosmetic bag'. I didn't pick up on it at the time… but later, I realised that I had never mentioned that it was 'quilted'. Gold, yes, but never quilted. Therefore, there was only one way you could have known that detail about the bag—if you had seen it yourself. And since Inspector Glenn had already told me that no one had been allowed into the room after the body had been found, that meant that you could only have seen it *before* the murder… which meant that *you* were the murderer hiding in the bathroom and *that's* when you must have seen the cosmetic bag."

"Well done," Derek Sutton said, a mocking smile playing around the corners of his mouth. "Yes, it was me in the bathroom. I had to do some quick thinking when that blasted idiot, Andrew Manning, suddenly appeared at the door. And then you turned up as well a few minutes later. In fact, I thought that trick with the electric toothbrush was pretty clever, if I do say so myself."

I looked at him in disgust. "Not clever enough," I said.

"Oh no?" He smiled again.

"No," I said. "When the police find out—"

"And why should the police know anything about it?"

"Because I'm going to tell them. When Inspector

Glenn gets back this afternoon, I'm going to tell him everything—"

"Oh, I think not, Miss Rose." He took a step towards me.

I backed away, suddenly realising that somehow, as we had been talking, he had manoeuvred us around so that I was standing with my back to the wall and he was between me and the ballroom entrance.

"D...don't come any closer," I said nervously, backing away. "Or I'll... I'll scream!"

"Scream away, Miss Rose," he said with a little laugh as he advanced towards me. "The main building is too far away and there's no one else here in the ballroom to hear you—"

"That's where you're wrong, young man!"

The familiar booming voice rang out across the ballroom. Derek Sutton whipped around, his mouth dropping open in horror as the Old Biddies marched into the ballroom, followed by Inspector Glenn.

Mabel came up to us, wagging her finger. "We heard everything you said, Mr Sutton—the full confession! It was a good thing that Inspector Glenn came back to the hotel early and an even better thing that we made him come to find Gemma with us."

Derek Sutton opened and closed his mouth but nothing came out.

The Old Biddies walked past him and came to fuss over me, while I sagged against the wall in relief. I couldn't quite believe what had happened. Derek

Sutton looked like he was having a hard time coping with reality as well, as Inspector Glenn handcuffed him and intoned:

"Derek Sutton, I'm arresting you for the murder of Jenn Murray. You do not have to say anything, but it may harm your defence if you do not mention when questioned, something which you later rely on in court..."

As he was being led away, Mabel called after him: "I still expect my discount on the ballroom!"

EPILOGUE

"Do you want to do it?" I asked nervously.

Cassie laughed. "Of course not, silly! It's *your* tearoom. Go on—open the door."

I took a deep breath, fingering the heavy brass key in my hand, then inserted it into the door. It turned with a rusty click and I gripped the doorknob and pushed. The door swung open with a faint creak and I stepped into the interior of the old Tudor building.

The place smelled slightly musty and there was dust everywhere but as Cassie strode over to the curtains and yanked them back, light flooded the place and I drew a breath of pleasure. Even with the hideous 70s décor scheme and cheap furniture, it was beautiful, full of Olde World charm. As dust motes danced in the beams of sunlight streaming in through the mullioned windows, I walked slowly around, admiring the exposed timber beams across the ceiling and the original 15th-century flagstone floors. On the far side of the room, the ugly screen had been removed and the rustic inglenook fireplace now dominated the wall.

I sighed happily. It really was like a dream come true.

And it was a dream that almost *hadn't* come true, I reminded myself wryly. It had been touch and go yesterday, getting the loan approval from the bank after news of Derek Sutton's arrest had finally been made public. And then it had been a race against time to get a bank draft to the original owners before they signed the deal with the Chinese.

But I had made it, I thought with a smile, as I looked down once more at the heavy brass key in my hand. It was a still a long road, I knew—it would be weeks before I could open for business, and in the meantime there would be renovations and redecorating, sourcing new furniture, working out the menu, finding a baker to make the delicious traditional British cakes and scones that I dreamed of...

As if on cue, the door to the tearoom swung open and Fletcher stepped in, the inevitable tool bag over one shoulder and a large flat package in his arms.

"Aha! Perfect timing, Fletcher!" cried Cassie, hurrying over to take the package from him, then turning to me with a smile. She held the package out to me.

"For you... a sort of tearoom-warming gift, I guess you could say." She chuckled.

Puzzled, I took the package from her. It was about the size of a very big tray, although much heavier. Slowly, I unwrapped the brown paper packaging, then caught my breath as I held up the thing to the light.

It was a hand-painted wooden sign—a shop sign— with a beautiful drawing of a quaint old stable door in the background and, in the foreground, a dainty china teapot with accompanying teacup. And underneath the picture, in flowing calligraphy, was the name: LITTLE STABLES TEAROOM.

"Oh Cass!" I said, tears springing to my eyes.

She enveloped me in a hug. "Congratulations, Gemma!"

I hugged her back, the tears spilling over now.

"Whoa... remember you're back in England now and you've got to act like a proper Brit. No excessive emotion in public," Cassie teased.

I laughed. "I don't know how to thank you. It's beautiful." I wiped the tears from my eyes.

"I'm glad you like it. I wasn't quite sure... but I could always paint you another one if you—"

"No, no, this one is perfect," I insisted. "I can't wait to hang it up."

"Well, Fletcher can help with that," said Cassie, nodding to the handyman who was standing shyly in the background. "That's why I got him to bring the sign—and all his tools."

"Thanks, that would be great." I smiled at Fletcher. Then I walked over and put a gentle hand on his arm. "But wait, before you do that... I wanted to ask you..." I took a deep breath. "Fletcher, would you be interested in coming to work for me here in the tearoom? As the baker?"

The big man looked at me in surprise. "Me?"

"Yes, your baking is wonderful and I'd love to have you on my team. It would be a full-time job so you probably couldn't do much of your handyman work anymore. But you like baking, don't you?"

"Yes, I love baking," said Fletcher simply.

"Then will you do it?"

He gave me a shy smile, then his forehead creased anxiously and he put a hand in his tool bag. There was a wriggle of movement and, a moment later, a little furry head popped out of the bag.

"*Meorrw?*" Muesli said, looking around the tearoom, her green eyes wide with curiosity.

"Can Muesli come too?" asked Fletcher.

I hesitated. Did I really have to have the tabby terror as well? Still, I could see that it was the only way Fletcher would agree.

"Well, I'd have to check with the Food Standards Agency and see what the laws are about having an animal in an eating establishment," I said cautiously. "But providing they're okay with it, then yes, Muesli can come too."

"*Meorrw!*" said Muesli, giving me a cheeky look of approval.

Then before anyone could stop her, she jumped out of the tool bag and began scampering about the place, her tail straight up and her whiskers quivering with excitement.

"Looks like Muesli's already decided to make herself at home," said Cassie with a laugh as the little cat hopped up to sit on the windowsill and tucked her tail around her paws.

I went over to join Muesli at the window and looked out onto the village. In the distance, the rolling hills of the Cotswolds stretched to the horizon and, closer in, the higgledy-piggledy rows of thatched-roof cottages with their stone walls glowing in the late autumn sunshine made an idyllic picture.

It was hard to believe that only a few days ago, I had been up to my neck in a murder investigation. Now that it was all over, I had to admit that it had been sort of... well, fun and exciting, in a way. But I didn't need any more of that, I told myself firmly. I was going to enjoy running a tearoom, with nothing more to worry about than how many scones one should serve and with which kind of jam and clotted cream. There'd be no more mysteries, murders, or secret alibis... no more sinister clues to follow or dangerous showdowns...

No, life was going to be peaceful now. After all, things like scones didn't get you killed, did they?

If only I knew...

A SCONE TO DIE FOR
(Oxford Tearoom Mysteries 1)

When an American tourist is murdered with a scone in Gemma Rose's quaint Oxfordshire tearoom, she suddenly finds herself apron-deep in a mystery involving long-buried secrets from Oxford's past.

Armed with her insider knowledge of the University and with the help of four nosy old ladies from the village (not to mention a cheeky little tabby cat named Muesli), Gemma sets out to solve the mystery—all while dealing with her matchmaking mother and the return of her old college love, Devlin O'Connor, now a dashing CID detective.

But with the body count rising and her business going bust, can Gemma find the killer before things turn to custard?

CHAPTER ONE

I never thought I'd end the week facing an American with a sharp knife.

It started normally enough, with the usual influx of tourists and visitors to our tiny Cotswolds' village of Meadowford-on-Smythe. Filled with winding cobbled lanes and pretty thatched cottages,

Meadowford was like a picture-perfect postcard of rural England. But quaint and gorgeous as the village was, it would probably never have got much notice if it hadn't sat on the outskirts of the most famous university city in the world.

Over nine million tourists came to visit Oxford each year, and after they'd posed for photos in the college quadrangles and wandered reverently through the cloisters of the oldest university in the English-speaking world, they drifted out into the surrounding Cotswolds countryside. Here, they would coo over the quaint antique shops and village markets, and look forward to rounding everything off with some authentic English "afternoon tea".

That's where I came in. Or rather, my new business: the Little Stables Tearoom. Offering the best in traditional English refreshments, from warm buttery scones with jam and clotted cream, to home-made sticky toffee pudding and hot cross buns, all served with fragrant Earl Grey or English Breakfast tea—*proper* leaf tea—in delicate bone china... my little tearoom was a must-stop on any visitor's itinerary.

Well, okay, right now, my little tearoom was more of a "must go next time"—but we all have to start somewhere, right?

And so far, things were looking pretty promising. I'd opened three weeks ago, just at the beginning of October and the start of the Michaelmas Term (a fancy name for the first term in the school year; hey, this is Oxford—at least it wasn't in Latin) and I'd been lucky to catch the end-of-the-summer tourist trade, as well as the flood of new students arriving with their families. My tearoom had even got a write-up in the local student magazine as one of the "Top Places to Take Your Parents" and looked set on its way to becoming a success.

And I desperately needed it to succeed. I'd given up a top executive job in Sydney—much to the horror of family and friends—on a crazy whim to come back home and follow this dream. I'd sunk every last penny of my savings into this place and I needed it to work. Besides, if my venture didn't become profitable soon, I'd never be able to afford a place of my own, and seriously, after being home for six weeks, I realised that moving back to live with your parents when you're twenty-nine is a fate worse than death.

But standing at the counter surveying my tearoom that Saturday morning, I was feeling happy and hopeful. It was still an hour till lunchtime but already the place was almost full. There was a warm cosy atmosphere, permeated by the cheerful hum of conversation, the dainty clink of china, and that gorgeous smell of fresh baking. People were poring over their menus, happily stuffing their faces, or pointing and looking around the room in admiration.

The tearoom was housed in a 15th-century Tudor building, with the distinctive dark half-timber framing and walls painted white. With its thatched roof and cross gables, it looked just like the quintessential English cottages featured on chocolate box tins. Inside, the period charm continued with flagstone floors and thick, exposed wood beams, matched by mullioned windows facing the street and an inglenook fireplace.

It hadn't looked like this when I took it over. The last owner had let things go badly, due to a combination of money troubles and personal lethargy (otherwise known as laziness), and it had taken a lot of effort and dedication—not to mention all my savings—to restore this place to its former glory. But looking around now, I felt as great a sense of achievement as I had done the day I graduated with a First from that world-famous university nearby.

I scanned the tables, noting that we were starting to get some "regulars" and feeling a rush of pleasure at the thought. Getting someone to try you once—especially when they were tired and hungry and just wanted somewhere to sit down—was one thing; getting them to add you to their weekly routine was a different honour altogether. Especially when that honour was handed out by the residents of Meadowford-on-Smythe who viewed all newcomers with deep suspicion.

Not that I was really a "newcomer"—I'd lived here as a little girl and, even after my family had moved to North Oxford in my teens, we'd always popped back to visit on school holidays and long weekends. But

I'd been gone long enough to be considered an "outsider" now and I knew that I would have to work hard to earn back my place in the village.

Still, it looked like I was taking my first steps. Sitting at the heavy oak table by the window were four little old ladies with their heads together, like a group of finicky hens deciding which unfortunate worm to peck first. Fluffy white hair, woolly cardigans, and spectacles perched on the ends of their noses... they looked like the stereotype of sweet, old grannies. But don't be fooled. These four could have given MI5 a run for their money. They made it their business to know everybody's business (that was just the basic service—interfering in other people's business was extra). It was rumoured that even the Mayor of Oxford was in their power.

But the fact that they were sitting in my tearoom was a good sign, I told myself hopefully. It meant that there was a chance I was being accepted and approved of. Then my heart sank as I saw one of them frown and point to an item on the menu. The other three leaned closer and there were ominous nods all around.

Uh-oh. I grabbed an order pad and hurried over to their table.

"Good morning, ladies." I pinned a bright smile to my face. "What can I get you today?"

They turned their heads in unison and looked up at me, four pairs of bright beady eyes and pursed lips.

"You're looking a bit peaky, Gemma," said Mabel Cooke in her booming voice. "Are you sure you're getting enough fibre, dear? There's a wonderful new type of bran you can take in the mornings, you know, to help you get 'regular'. Dr Foster recommended it to me. Just a spoon on your cereal and you'll be in the loo, regular as clockwork. Works marvellously to clear you out." She leaned closer and added in a stage whisper, which was loud enough for the entire room to hear, "*So* much cheaper than that colon irritation thing they do, dear."

I saw the couple at the next table turn wide eyes on me and felt myself flushing. "Er... thank you, Mrs Cooke. Now, can I take—"

"I saw your mother in Oxford yesterday," Glenda Bailey spoke up from across the table. As usual, she was wearing bright pink lipstick, which clashed badly with the rouge on her cheeks, but somehow the overall effect was charming. Glenda was eighty going on eighteen, with a coquettish manner that went perfectly with her girlish looks. "Has she had her hair done recently?"

To be honest, I had no idea. I had only been back six weeks and I thought my mother looked pretty much the same. But I suppose her hair was in a different style to the last time I'd returned to England.

"Er... yes, I think so."

Glenda clucked her tongue and fluttered her eyelashes in distress. "Oh, it was shocking. So flat and shapeless. I suppose she went to one of those fancy new hairdressers in Oxford?"

"I... I think she did."

There were gasps from around the table.

"She should have come to Bridget here in the village," said Mabel disapprovingly. "Nobody can do a wash and blow dry like our Bridget. She even gave me a blue rinse for free the last time I was there." She patted her head with satisfaction, then turned back to me with a scowl. "Really, Gemma! Young hairdressers nowadays know nothing about lift and volume. I don't know why your mother is going to these fancy new hair salons."

Maybe because not everyone wants to walk around wearing a cotton wool helmet on their heads, I thought, but I bit back the retort.

"It's because they have no concept of 'staying power'," Florence Doyle spoke up. Her simple, placid face was unusually earnest. "They've never been through the war and have no idea of rationing. They don't know how to make things last as long as possible. People wash their hair so frequently these days." She gave a shudder.

"Well, a wash and set once a week was good enough for my mother and it's good enough for me," said Mabel with an emphatic nod. She eyed me suspiciously. "How often do you wash your hair, Gemma?"

"I... um... only when I need to," I stammered, thinking guiltily of my daily shower and shampoo.

With a determined effort, I changed the subject. "What would you like to order for morning tea?"

"I'd like some of your delicious warm scones with jam and clotted cream—and a pot of English Breakfast, please," Ethel Webb spoke up.

The quietest of the group, Ethel was a kindly, absent-minded spinster who used to be the librarian at the local library until she retired a few years ago. I remembered her gentle face smiling at me as she stamped the return date on my books when I was a little girl.

She gave me that same gentle smile now. "And I think you've done a lovely job with the tearoom, Gemma. I'm really proud of you."

I looked at her in surprise, a sudden tightness coming to my throat. Since announcing my decision to ditch my high-flying corporate career for a village tearoom, the reactions I'd received had ranged from aghast disbelief to horrified disapproval. I hadn't realised until now how much a bit of support meant to me.

"Thank you..." I said, blinking rapidly. "Thank you, Miss Webb. I... I can't tell you how much I appreciate your words."

Her eyes twinkled at me. "Now that you're nearly thirty, Gemma, do you think you could call me Ethel, dear? I'm not behind the library desk anymore, you know."

I returned her smile. "I'll try, Miss... Ethel."

I managed to take the rest of the orders without

further comment on my bowels, my mother's hair follicles or the young generation's lack of economy, and hurried back to the counter in relief. My best friend, Cassie, met me on the way. She had been looking after a large group of American tourists, which had just arrived by coach and was now settled in the tables along the far wall.

"Looks like you survived another encounter with the Old Biddies," she said with a grin as we both rounded the counter.

I rolled my eyes. "If I have to hear one more thing about Mabel's 'regular' bowel habits, I think I'm going to take a running jump."

"You'll get no sympathy from me," said Cassie. "You've only had to put up with them for three weeks so far. I've been putting up with them for the past eight years while you've been gallivanting off Down Under."

Cassie and I had known each other from the time we both believed in Santa Claus. That moment when we'd first sat down next to each other in the classroom of our village school had been the start of an unexpected but wonderful friendship. Unexpected because you couldn't have found two people more un-alike than Cassie and me. She was one of five siblings in a large, rowdy family where everyone talked constantly—when they weren't singing, dancing, painting, or sculpting—and the house was in a constant state of cluttered chaos. Cassie's parents were "artists" in the true sense of the word and believed that the most important things in life were creative freedom and personal expression. It was no surprise that Cassie had done Fine Art at Oxford.

I, meanwhile, was the only child of an upper-middle-class household where nobody spoke at any volume above a well-modulated murmur and certainly never with excessive emotion. My house was always a perfectly ordered sanctuary of cream furniture and matching curtains. My parents were "British" in the true sense of the word and believed that the most important things in life were a stiff upper lip and correct etiquette. You couldn't do "Ladylike Decorum" as a degree at Oxford so my mother had had to settle for me doing English Language and Literature.

Like most artists, Cassie worked a series of part-time jobs to help make ends meet. When she learned about my plans to return to Meadowford-on-Smythe and re-open the tearoom, it had taken very little to convince her to ditch her usual day job and come work with me. In fact, her past waitressing experience had been invaluable. Even now, I watched in admiration as she expertly balanced several plates laden with scones, cheesecake, and crumpets—as well as a pot of tea and two teacups—and started to make her way to the table of Japanese tourists by the door.

A strange snapping noise caught my attention and I turned towards the sound. It was coming from a large man who seemed to be part of the tour group that had just come in. He was sitting alone at a table at the edge of the group and had his left hand in the air, snapping it impatiently, like someone calling a disobedient dog. I frowned at his rudeness, but reminded myself that I was in the hospitality industry now. *Professional, friendly service no matter what.* I took a deep breath and went over to him.

"Can I help you, sir?"

"Yeah, I wanna glass of water."

He had a strong American accent and an aggressive manner, which put me instantly on edge, but I kept my smile in place.

"Certainly." I started to turn away but paused as he spoke again.

"Wait—is it tap? I only drink filtered water."

"I'm afraid we don't have a filter, sir. It's plain tap water. But it's very safe to drink tap water in the U.K. We do have bottled water on the menu, if you prefer."

He scowled. "What a rip-off. Water should be free."

I stifled a sigh. "You can certainly have water for free, but it'll be tap water. We have to pay for the bottled water so I have to charge you for that."

"All right, all right…" He waved a hand. "Get me a glass of tap water. And put some ice in it."

I turned to go but was stopped again by his voice.

"Hey, by the way, the service is terrible. I've been sitting here forever and no one's come to take my order!"

I stared at him, wondering if he was serious.

Surely he realised that he had only just come in a few minutes ago? The rest of the group were still looking at their menus. One of the women in the group, sitting at the next table with her little boy, met my eyes and gave me a sympathetic smile. I took a deep breath and let it out through my nose.

"I'll just grab my order pad, sir."

"Yeah, well, be quick about it. I haven't got all day."

Gritting my teeth, I headed back to the counter. My mood was not improved when I got there to find Cassie with an exasperated look on her face.

"The shop's empty again."

"Arrrrgghh!" I said under my breath. "Muesli, I'm going to kill you!"

No, I don't have an abnormal hatred of cereals. Muesli is a cat and, like all cats, she delights in doing the exact opposite of what you want. The Food Standards Agency inspector had been adamant: the only way I'd be allowed to have a cat on the premises was if it stayed out of the kitchen and dining areas. *Easy*, I'd thought. *I'll just keep Muesli in the extension where we had a little shop selling Oxford souvenirs and English tea paraphernalia.* The fact that I thought of the words "easy" and "cat" in the same sentence probably tells you that I don't know much about felines.

Okay, I'll be the first to admit—I've always been more of a dog person. I think cats are fascinating and beautiful and look great on greeting cards. But not on my lap leaving hairs everywhere and certainly not in my tearoom, getting under everyone's feet. So why, you wonder, is the tabby terror even here? Well, she came as a packaged deal with my chef. And Fletcher Wilson is a *magician* with a mixer and a spatula. Trust me, once you've tasted his sticky toffee pudding, you'd be ready to give him your first born child. So agreeing to let him have his cat with him at work seemed like a small price to pay in exchange for his culinary expertise.

The problem was, I hadn't counted on the cat being quite so sociable. Or such a great escape artist. Muesli had quickly decided that there was no way she was going to remain in the shop area when all the real fun was going on here in the dining room and she made it her life's mission to escape at any opportunity. I couldn't really blame her. In fact, I felt guilty every time I saw that little tabby face—with her pink nose pressed up to the glass—peering wistfully through the door that separated the shop from the dining room. But food hygiene laws were one thing I couldn't ignore if I didn't want to lose my licence.

"One of the Japanese tourists must have gone in the shop to check out some of the stuff and she slipped out when they opened the door," commented Cassie.

I sighed and scanned the room, looking for a little tabby shape between the tables. I couldn't see her. I crouched down to get a better view. All I could see was a forest of legs... I bit my lip. *Where was that cat?*

I had to find her before any of the customers noticed her loose in here. The last thing I needed was for Mabel and her cronies to discover my Food Standards violation; the news would be halfway across Oxfordshire before the day ended.

"Hey! Can I get some service around here?" came an irate American voice.

I straightened up hurriedly. *Oh God, I'd forgotten about Mr Charming.* I gave Cassie a harassed look. "Keep looking for her, will you?"

I grabbed the order pad—then, on an impulse, also picked up a plate of fresh blackberry cheesecake, which had just come through the hatch from the kitchen. *Well, they did say the way to a man's heart was through his stomach.* I added a knife and fork, and a dollop of cream, then walked over and set it down in front of him.

"Sorry for the wait, sir. Compliments of the house. This is one of our specialties."

"Huh." He looked surprised. He picked up the fork and cut the corner off the soft, creamy cake, putting it cautiously into his mouth. His eyes glazed over slightly and his face softened. "Say... this is not bad."

I suppressed the urge to roll my eyes. Coming from him, that was probably considered high praise. Still, trying to be charitable, I told myself that maybe he was just one of those people who got really grouchy when hungry. I observed him surreptitiously as I took his order. He was a large, thickset man, with a blocky, almost square-shaped head, fleshy cheeks and prominent ears. His mouth drooped slightly on one side as he talked—the result of a stroke?—and I put him in his early forties, though he looked older. He seemed slightly incongruous sitting there with the other tourists. He was certainly dressed like a tourist in chinos, a loud shirt, and sports jacket, and he had a sort of knapsack on the chair next to him, but somehow he didn't quite fit in.

"...and I gotta have the bread soft, d'you hear? I don't want any hard crusts on the sandwiches."

"All our tea sandwiches are made the traditional way with untoasted bread and the crusts cut off, so they're all very soft to eat," I assured him. I noticed the tourist map of Oxford spread out on the table in front of him and gave him a polite smile. "Visiting Oxford, sir?"

"What?" He glanced down at the map. "Oh... oh, yeah." He gave me a sheepish grin. "Yeah, first-time visitor here; never been to Oxford before. Gotta figure out how to get around. Say, you know how long it takes to walk from the Bodleian Library to Magdalen College?"

"No more than ten or fifteen minutes, I should think. You can take the shortcut through Catte Street onto High Street, and then just turn left and walk straight down to the bridge."

"Catte Street... that comes out opposite the bank, doesn't it?"

I frowned. "You mean, the Old Bank Hotel?"

He blinked and a look of confusion flashed across

his face, to be replaced quickly by a bland smile. "Sure, yeah, that's what I mean." He folded up the map. "Well, thanks for that. You gotta restroom here?"

I directed him to the door beside the shop, then hurried back to the counter to put his order through. I could hear raised voices in the kitchen and winced. I wondered if Cassie was telling Fletcher about his missing cat. I hoped it wouldn't upset him too much. Fletcher was… "sensitive", for want of a better word. He was painfully shy and didn't relate to people like most of us did—in fact, he found it difficult to even make eye contact when he spoke to you. Animals seemed to be the only thing that helped him come out of his shell and I knew that having Muesli here played a big role in calming his nerves and helping him cope with things.

Remembering the request for water, I hurriedly poured a glass and added a few ice-cubes, then took it back to the American man's table. As I was putting it down, the little boy at the next table jumped up with a yell and jostled my elbow. Water sloshed out of the glass and onto the man's knapsack.

"Blast!" I muttered.

"Oh, I'm so sorry!" said the woman at the next table. "Hunter, apologise to the lady."

I gave the little boy a distracted smile. "That's okay. It was an accident."

I set the glass down and picked up the knapsack, trying to shake the water off. It was unzipped and a lot of water had spilled onto a folder inside. I hesitated a second, then pulled the folder out and grabbed a napkin from the holder on the table to mop up the moisture. My heart sank as I saw that water had seeped into the folder and wet the sheaf of papers inside. I could just imagine the American's reaction when he came out and saw what had happened.

Hastily, I pulled out the sheets and dabbed at them with more napkins. The water had soaked through the first page. I hoped it wasn't anything important. It had the look of an official letter, with the *University of Oxford* letterhead at the top, but what I was more worried about was the bottom where the signature—obviously done in fountain pen—had smeared across the page. I dabbed at it, thinking to myself frantically: most signatures were illegible anyway, weren't they? This one, for instance, you could hardly make out what the name was. It looked like a "G" and then "Hayes" or "Hughes", but in any case—

"WHAT THE HELL DO YOU THINK YOU'RE DOING?"

I gasped as a hand grabbed my wrist and yanked me back from the table. Conversation at the next table ceased and the whole room went silent as everyone turned to stare. The American towered over me, one hand clamped on my wrist, the other holding something that gleamed dully. My eyes widened as I realised that it was a knife.

THE OXFORD TEAROOM MYSTERIES

All-Butter ShortDead (Prequel)
A Scone to Die For (Book 1)
Tea with Milk and Murder (Book 2)
Two Down, Bun To Go (Book 3)
Till Death Do Us Tart (Book 4)
Muffins and Mourning Tea (Book 5)
Four Puddings and a Funeral (Book 6)
Another One Bites the Crust (Book 7)
Apple Strudel Alibi (Book 8)
The Dough Must Go On (Book 9)
The Mousse Wonderful Time of Year (Book 10)

For other books by H.Y. Hanna,

please visit her website:

www.hyhanna.com

GLOSSARY OF BRITISH TERMS

** In British English, the past participle of forget is "forgot", not "forgotten", e.g. *I had forgot the date.* Similarly, we use "disorientated" instead of "disoriented".

Allotment – a plot of land which can be rented on an individual basis, to grow your own plants and vegetables

Biscuit – small, hard, baked product, either savoury or sweet *(American: cookies. What is called a "biscuit" in the U.S. is more similar to the English scone)*

Blimey – an expression of astonishment

Bloody – very common adjective used as an intensifier for both positive and negative qualities (e.g. "bloody awful" and "bloody wonderful"), often used to express shock or disbelief ("Bloody Hell!")

Bobby – affectionate slang term for a policeman; derived from the nickname for Sir Robert Peel, the founder of the Metropolitan Police. Often used in the phrase: "village bobby" to refer to the local community police officer who looks after small

English villages.

Bollocks! – an exclamation of annoyance

Carpark – a place to park vehicles *(American: parking lot)*

Chips - thin, long rectangular pieces of deep-fried potato (American: fries)

Cuppa – slang term for "a cup of tea"

Dishy – handsome, attractive (used for men)

Gormless – lacking sense, very foolish

Ladybird – a small beetle with a distinctive red coat covered in white spots *(American: ladybug)*

Lift – a compartment in a shaft which is used to raise and lower people to different levels *(America: elevator)*

Plonker – an annoying idiot

Poncy – pretentious, affected

Rotter - someone to be regarded with contempt

Run-in – a confrontation

Sod off – "get lost", go away, stop bothering me; milder version of the phrase using the F-word.

Stuffed – to be in big trouble, to be "done for"

Tuck into – to eat with great enthusiasm

Arvo (Australian) – afternoon

Barbie (Australian) – barbecue

Nipper (Australian) – a small child

***

Special terms used in Oxford University:

College - one of thirty or so institutions that make up the University; all students and academic staff have to be affiliated with a college and most of your life revolves around your own college: studying, dining, socialising. You are, in effect, a member of a College much more than a member of the University. College loyalties can be fierce and there is often friendly rivalry between nearby colleges. The colleges also compete with each other in various University sporting events.

Fellow – a member of the academic staff / governing body of a college *(equivalent to "faculty member" in the U.S.)* – basically refers to a college's tutors. "Don" comes from the Latin, *dominus*—meaning lord, master.

Gown – formal black academic robe worn by students and staff, particularly during Formal Hall, Examinations and during Matriculation and Graduation. There are various types of gowns: the simplest is the short, sleeveless Commoner gown which all Freshers start with; if you have shown outstanding achievement in your first year, you then receive a University scholarship and can change to the longer, bat-winged Scholar's gown.

Porter's Lodge – a room next to the college gates which holds the porters' offices and also the "pigeon holes"—cubby holes where the internal University mail is placed and notes for students can be left by their friends.

Sub-fusc – full academic dress worn during all formal University ceremonies, including

Examinations, Matriculation and Graduation; consists of your gown, mortar board and for men, a dark suit with a white collared shirt, bow tie and black shoes, for women, a dark skirt with white collared shirt, black ribbon and black shoes and stockings.

ABOUT THE AUTHOR

USA Today bestselling author H.Y. Hanna writes fun cozy mysteries filled with quirky characters, lots of laughs, clever twists—and cats with big personalities! She is known for bringing wonderful settings to life, whether it's the historic city of Oxford, the beautiful English Cotswolds or the sunny beaches of coastal Florida.

After graduating from Oxford University, Hsin-Yi tried her hand at a variety of jobs, including advertising, modelling, teaching English and dog training... before returning to her first love: writing. She worked as a freelance writer for several years and has won awards for her poetry, short stories and journalism.

Hsin-Yi was born in Taiwan and has been a globe-trotter all her life—living in a variety of cultures, from Dubai to Auckland, London to New Jersey—but is now happily settled in Perth, Western Australia, with her husband and a rescue kitty named Muesli. You can learn more about her and her books at: www.hyhanna.com.

Join her Readers' Club Newsletter to get updates on new releases, exclusive giveaways and other book news!

https://www.hyhanna.com/newsletter

ACKNOWLEDGMENTS

Thank you to Basma Alwesh and Jenn Roseton for their very helpful feedback in beta-reading this story, and a special thanks to Connie Leap for her help with proofreading the manuscript.

And to my wonderful husband—for his encouragement, support, endless patience and humour—from the practical things, like taking care of household chores so that I have more time to write, to always offering a listening ear and a shoulder to cry on. He is one man in a million.

Printed in Great Britain
by Amazon

36891746R00108